I0788918

RANSOME

A FROZEN PLANET PREQUEL

DAVID W, ADAMS

ISBN:
978-1-916582-57-6 [Paperback]
978-1-916582-56-9 [eBook]
978-1-916582-58-3 [Hardcover]

ECHO ON PUBLICATIONS

The following story contains some potentially triggering themes. Whilst not as gruesome as *Horizon* was, or as horrific as *Emergence* is going to be, there are still themes which may cause upset. They are as follows:

- Graphic descriptions of injury
- Graphic depictions of dead bodies
- Descriptions of mutilation
- Body horror
- Medical experimentation
- Mental manipulation

If you find any more triggering themes in the book, please let me know and I will update the list accordingly. Your mental health is always the priority, so take breaks where needed. And keep reminding yourself, it's only a book.

For Alexia and Iain,
Horizon was in my opinion my best work, and to say you agreed with
me would be an understatement.
I felt I owed you a thank you. So here it is.

PROLOGUE

Space is nothing but a graveyard.

How true those words rang now. As the crimson pool beneath Lieutenant Joshua Knight's now lifeless body began to expand and drip down the edge of the deck plate, Admiral Harry Ransome clenched his fists so tightly that they almost glowed under the ominous hue of the red emergency lights on the bridge.

"I won't do it," he growled. "You're not having my ship."

A small sigh came from the figure looming behind him as they slowly lowered the disruptor, the tip still glowing from the burst of energy that had moments before carved a hole through his communications officer.

"Harry, Harry, Harry. Surely you have figured this out by now? You cannot win here. You have lost. Perhaps your people should have remained in their solar system where they belong. It's not safe out here."

The voice, once calm and soothing in any situation to Harry Ransome, now bled with venom and toxicity. A fool. He had been nothing but a fool. He glanced at the pre-prepared speech still displayed in front of him, written by his captors. He was to deliver this message to the people of Earth urging them not to come looking for the *Odyssey* and her crew. It would effectively be a death sentence for humanity, but the violence on display before the Admiral was undeniable. Four officers lay dead in various points around the bridge. Each refusal had been met with an execution. Not that he had many crew members left. Of the one thousand souls who had left Earth almost a decade ago, only fifty-two now remained. He still heard their screams in his nightmares. *She* had made sure of that.

"Why do you need the *Odyssey*?" he asked as he tilted his head slightly to try and get a better view of the threat he was facing. "You were able to infiltrate my crew without a vast ship, no shots were fired. So it can't be for warfare. Although I doubt you've enough lackeys to commit the genocide you asked me to complete."

The associate of the leader had an itchy trigger finger, seemingly only a whisper away from burning a hole through someone else. Seemingly sensing his anxiety, the leader gestured to him to lower his weapon. Whatever happened here, they needed Harry alive. And preferably as many of his crew as possible. Although if he didn't cooperate soon, that number would dwindle rapidly.

"You have something we need," came the reply. "Something we can't replicate."

Harry found that extremely hard to believe. These people were clearly in possession of technology far in advance of their own, not to mention their telepathic abilities. And so he asked the question, he immediately regretted the answer to.

"And just what would that be?"

Stepping forward out of the shadows and lowering her hood, the leader simply smiled, the red lights creating a purple glow around her bright blue hair.

"Humanity."

EMERGENCY TRANSMISSION RECEIVED

Utopia secure channel Alpha-Tango-4-7.

Location : Unknown.

Source of transmission : Unknown.

Identifier code : USS Odyssey.

Commander : Admiral Harry Ransome.

Message received : 02:47, Nov 7 2342

Message playback :

"To anyone in the Sol System, any humans that can hear me. This is Admiral Harry Ransome, on board the Earth vessel Odyssey. We were dispatched by our people almost a decade ago to search for a new home for our people and explore the galaxy. Two months into our journey, we encountered a species called the Darla. They were in a similar state to ourselves, seeking a new home. They told us about a phenomenon they'd become aware of called The Horizon. The Darla gave us a fantastical tale of how this energy nebula would transport you back in time to a place where you were at your happiest. Naturally, as a military man, I dismissed the notion as having no

scientific grounding whatsoever. But my crew began to interact with the Darla, and the more they did so, the more they were convinced The Horizon existed. Fights began breaking out amongst senior officers, and in little to no time, we had our first death on board.

I don't know what possessed me to seek out this place. The Darla appeared to have some kind of telepathic influence over us, and even though I knew it meant we would miss our check in with our monthly transmission to Earth, I ordered us to set course.

Do not come looking for us.

It is too late for us.

Those who left are gone. They entered the Expanse, and they never came back. I heard their screams over the communications channels as if they were inside my own head. Others took the escape pods and launched into the darkness.

There's nothing here.

Space is nothing but a graveyard.

You can fool yourself into thinking it is a magical and wondrous place full of intrigue and exploration, but in reality it was nothing but death and emptiness surrounded in shadows and blood.

We were wrong. I was wrong.

I have only fifty-two crew left on board. I'm turning the Odyssey around and heading for the nearest space station. It's not far from here. Seems to be a traders place of business. Maybe we can barter our way to a nearby home for those of us that are left.

Maybe one day, we will find our way back to you."

ONE

Harry Ransome had enlisted in the Utopia programme for one purpose and one purpose alone. Exploration. Although he was being billed as the founder of the mission, it was simply a press requirement. In truth, there had been four people involved in setting up the plans and putting the starships into production. With a hero figurehead needed to be the face of Utopia, Harry was chosen for his dedication to duty and his war record. That in itself was a joke. He had often thought to himself, if the people of Earth truly knew what he had done in battle, then they would have him shot. And for what? A woman. Weakness. To remain in a singular moment of happiness. Something which had long left him at home.

Harry's wife, Annette, had instructed him to leave the family home long before he met the President of Earth, but they had always labelled themselves as 'separated' rather than apart, and neither of them had actually filed for divorce. Harry had often glanced down at his gold wedding band, twirling it on his finger, wishing everything could go back to the way it was before. Before all the fighting, before all of the climate emergencies, before he met... her.

Utopia was his way out. Running away from all of his problems, and saving humanity at the same time. He knew the planet of Earth didn't have long left. Every one of the ship Captains knew it. Regardless of what they said to the media or the top brass, they knew that once they left, they would never come back. In truth, they were abandoning the rest of humanity to their doom. But not Harry. He was determined to find a new home, and he would find a way back. He would right all of the wrongs he had done and be lauded for a new truth. One in which he hadn't massacred millions of indigenous peoples on both Mars and Jupiter. A new truth where he wasn't controlled by... her.

And what a control it was. Drusilla had utilised a previously unknown ability to manipulate her way into the hierarchy of Earth's government and taken the top spot all to herself. She was a fierce warrior in battle, but more often than not, she simply manipulated people's minds into doing her bidding. As far as Harry knew, he was the only one she had outwardly revealed this ability to. The rest of the planet assumed she was fully human. It was Drusilla who had convinced Earth's forces to quash the rebellion on Mars to keep mankind safe. The rebellion that was of course simply an implanted memory slipped into the right heads. Harry was encapsulated by both her beauty and her mere presence. If a person's aura was truly visible, she would have glowed like an angel to him. His entire body seemed to be transported to another plain of existence when she was in reach of him, and a euphoria comforted him like a blanket. More often than not, the effect would also remove the memory of what he had done whilst in his trance like state, and he would have to learn the horrors afterwards.

Jupiter had been next. But this one was personal for Drusilla. She ordered more forces than anyone had thought necessary to launch an attack on the native species of the planet, the Darla. They too were a telepathic race, but were clearly not of human origin, distinguishable by the markers on their faces. Many of them had fled, but three-quarters of their population were destroyed at the hands of Harry and Drusilla.

Of course during the wars, Drusilla was not yet in her high and mighty role. No, that came later, when she could combine her telepathic manipulation with her own battle records to create an undefeatable motion. She won the vote with over ninety-six percent. Harry was then slipped into his position, Utopia was created, and the next thing Harry knew, she was giving him a tour of the now ready for launch *USS Odyssey*.

"We can't keep doing this Dru," Harry spoke softly as he pulled his clothes from the nearby desk where he had left them the night before.

"You do not wish to be with me?" she asked with a tone that sounded more threatening than hurt by his words.

"No. This isn't real. This whole sensation, it's incredible, yes I admit. But it's all a facsimile of the real thing. You don't love me. And I don't love you. It's all manipulation. And it needs to stop."

Even Harry was surprised at his own words. Never before had he resisted Drusilla as much as he now was. He was almost too fearful to turn his back and face her, should she ensnare his attention once more.

"And yet, you cannot seem to break away."

Drusilla had now risen from the bed, and was also reaching towards her discarded clothing. Harry could not stop himself from admiring the sheer beauty of the woman as she slid the straps of her dress back over her shoulders. But he was right. The mission ahead was too important for distractions. She had to know that.

"Then it is a good thing I am leaving. What will you do?" he asked, genuinely curious.

"I will return to our people. They need their leader now more than ever. I can give them peace. In time, it may be the only thing I can offer them. Should you fail."

Harry put down the sonic shaver he was reaching for and turned to face her with fury in his eyes.

"You don't think I can do this without you, do you?"

Drusilla said nothing.

"You really do think all of this is down to you, and not the hard work of every man and woman in this programme!"

Drusilla made for the door.

"Goodbye Harry. Watch yourself out there. It's not safe. I should know."

And just like that, she was gone, the whoosh of the door the only sound as it closed, leaving Admiral Harry Ransome standing alone in his new quarters, the stars twinkling behind him beyond the tall and curving windows.

TWO

Harry often did as he was doing at this very moment. He sat at his desk, computer terminal activated, scrolling through the list of battle achievements listed from the conflict on Jupiter. Battle achievements. Commendations. Hero's welcomes upon their return. All a lie. The truth was far more nefarious. Drusilla had been on the losing end of a war with the Darla over three centuries earlier. Humans were still very much stuck in their own orbit and had no idea what was raging on the far side of the Sol System. In truth, the Darla had been the aggressors at the beginning. They had been the ones to venture out looking to expand amongst the stars, and came upon Drusilla's home world. And it had been *them* who had attacked Drusilla's father out of fear. They fled the planet and returned to Jupiter, hiding underground. But the damage was done. Drusilla's anger was awoken, and there was no amount of water that could extinguish that fire. It took her two hundred years to travel to Earth, and almost another hundred to manipulate her way into exacting her revenge. And Harry had helped her pull the trigger.

His nightmares were frequent, and detailed. The faces of the children of Jupiter as he burrowed an energy beam through their skull, no emotion on his own face, fully under the control of his manipulator. There was no mercy shown and no quarter given. Only death. Harry was convinced that Earth's continued demise was simply opportune timing for Drusilla to put together the Utopia mission. The tag line was very catchy.

'To allow the flower of humanity to blossom amongst the stars.'

The slogan was printed everywhere. Buildings, conference halls, vehicles, television, anywhere the message could be beamed into the minds of the people. Eventually, when it became known that Harry as military commander was brought on board, the slogan was changed to one more befitting potential recruitment.

'To find salvation amongst the stars.'

It worked. By that point, humanity was desperate and all efforts were made to push ahead with the program. The more militaristic slogan garnered more bodies willing to put it all on the line to save their people, and the vessels were created six years ahead of schedule.

But Harry knew why Drusilla wanted this mission to go ahead so badly. She wanted the Darla refugees destroyed. Wherever they had fled to, wherever they had gone, space itself would not be big enough or dark enough to hide them from her. Which made Harry all the more nervous about why he was planning to do next.

"Bridge to Admiral Ransome."

Harry closed down his monitor, and tapped the communication device which was sewn onto the cuff of his wrist.

"Go ahead."

"Engineering reports the *Odyssey* is ready to depart, Sir."

"Understood Ensign. I'll be right out."

A second tap to the wrist closed the channel, and Harry stood, swept his blue and red uniform jacket from the back of his chair, and as he studied himself in the reflection of his mirror, he paused for a moment.

"Here we go, Harry. No turning back now. For humanity."

Brushing the creases from his uniform, he took a deep breath and strode out of his quarters, stopping just shy of the bridge doors. He glanced upwards as if talking to an invisible person.

"Computer, locate President Drusilla."

A momentary pause before an acknowledging chime.

"President Drusilla is not aboard the USS Odyssey."

"Perfect."

Harry pushed forward, the doors moving apart ahead of him, revealing the brand new command centre to the flagship of the Utopia fleet. Although he had seen the bridge on the tour with Drusilla, this was the first time he had seen the room fully engaged. It took his breath away. Finally, he was going to be doing what he always wanted to do as a child. Be an explorer. While the stakes were high and there were outside influences, Harry had already decided that this is where it ended.

This is where he told Drusilla to go fuck herself.

THREE

There would be no reason for him to come back, she knew that. The relationship between him and his wife had long since been destroyed. There was neither any love lost between him and his son. But then again, it never hurt to make sure.

As Drusilla wiped the blood from her crystal blade, she noticed the puddle had now reached her foot, staining her light grey footwear.

"Damn humans. Your blood never comes out. Still, I wonder if Mrs Harry Ransome has some delightful shoes in her closet I could borrow. She isn't going to need them, after all."

The visit had been unprompted. Drusilla had watched the *Odyssey,* and three of the other ships leave orbit from the space dock, and it had occurred to her that although Harry's destination was always going to be in front of him, she would help him along by removing any temptation to return. Nothing could distract him from hunting down the Darla. And of course when the President of Earth knocks on your door, you don't slam the door in her face.

Unfortunately for Annette Ransome and her son Finlay, the

pretence of friendship was a very well worn mask. Being in the public eye for as many years as they had been, they had almost grown an automatic skin that responded to pleasantries and greetings almost without them even noticing it. It wasn't until Annette had gone to replicate some tea, that she had heard the sound of Finlay choking on his own blood. A blink of an eye later, and the same blade of crystal which had sliced her son's throat from ear to ear had flown through the air and embedded itself dead centre in her jugular, impaling her against the refrigerator, tea cascading over the edge of the counter.

"Much better."

Drusilla was now sporting a pair of diamond blue heels that Harry had bought Annette for their last anniversary. It had indeed been their last for a variety of reasons, one of which was the work of the President.

"You know my dear, I often wondered if he was happy that he had gotten away from you. He seemed so much happier with me. Certainly more enthusiastic. But there was always a part of him that loved you. A small percentage of his willpower, trying to drag him back to you. Pathetic really. At least now I have removed that temptation for him. Consider this a release from the horror of what is to befall this place."

A small tap on the shoulder of the two presidential guards outside the house, and their eyes glazed over immediately.

"Dispose of the wife and child. Make it look like an accident."

A simple nod from each of them, and they disappeared into the house, the door closing behind them. Drusilla stepped into her transportation pod, and closed the door.

"Pod, return me to the White House."

"Destination set, President Drusilla. ETA six minutes."

It was during these small travels between locations that Drusilla allowed her own mind to wander. She reflected on her homeworld, her family, and how happy she had been all those centuries ago. Then inevitably, her mind would switch to the image of her father being shot dead by Darla invaders. They had killed more than one of her family that night. Her mother, overcome with grief had taken her own life the following week, and her brother the month afterwards. She had known she would have to be stronger than all of those she loved to find those responsible. And when she did, she would not simply take the life of her father's killer. She would take *everything* from them.

She chuckled to herself as she recalled the destruction of Jupiter. Some wars were over resources, some over territory. But sometimes, there was nothing more complicated about a war than simple revenge. No double crossing, no second guessing. Simple revenge.

Her grandfather had been the one to tell Drusilla after the loss of her family that when someone wrongs you in this life, it is your honour bound duty to right that wrong. It was his crystal blade she now carried. She had no way of learning if he was even still alive. Drusilla's people were extremely long lived, with lifespans of up to twelve-hundred years. But at the time of her leaving their home, he was already over a thousand years old. She mourned for him briefly, and a tear threatened to escape from her cobalt blue eyes. Then the pod interrupted her thought process, and she placed her protective barriers back up in her mind.

"Destination achieved, President Drusilla."

She stepped out of the pod, and was immediately surrounded by White House staff. They were very attentive, even without any extra manipulation on her part, and she found herself feeling more and more comfortable the longer she had reigned. The building, however, had never been to her taste. No place of power had been built on any world without standing on the back of slaves, and she knew the American fortress at the heart of Washington D.C. was no different. One of her first acts as President had been to have the entire building reconstructed from new materials, on what was formerly the Spanish coastline. She kept the name for familiarity, but she was the President of Earth. Not of America. Once the new building was complete on the outskirts of Benalmadena, she ordered the original White House to be destroyed.

Most of the Utopia facilities were now in mainland Spain. The families of those onboard the ships were almost exclusively stationed there. They believed it was one of the few countries that still had a wide abundance of clean air. In reality, it was Drusilla's way of keeping them all under the thumb. Company owned housing, company provided meals, and clothes, and everything else they could possibly need. One day, a small additive in their company supplied cups of coffee, and they'd relinquish their lives without ever knowing that anything was wrong.

That was another mantra she had brought in. Don't question the company. Whatever the question, the answer would always be the same. For the good of humanity. Same answer every time, so don't ask. Drusilla walked the long trek from the lawn, through the ground floor, and up to her private elevator. She never allowed anyone else access to her living accommodation. This was actually written into law years earlier. Anyone caught in her private residence would be executed without trial. Did people question such a barbaric rule? Of course not. Why? Because anyone who did, was swiftly executed. Without trial. Telepathy and power. A terrifying combination.

Closing the door to her suite, she changed out of her visiting attire, and the stolen shoes, and slipped into her favourite loungewear. It had been her mother's and was made of the finest silk, embroidered with golden symbols of her people. It brought her comfort when she was alone, and allowed her to sleep at night without too much disturbance.

Pouring herself a large glass of whiskey (another favourite she had made sure was stacked on a ship ready to depart any minute), she tapped an access code into a seemingly unspectacular panel of wood, the numbers only illuminating *after* being pressed. The wall behind the drinks cabinet then slid backwards by several inches, before rotating one-hundred-and-eighty degrees, revealing a hidden doorway into another room. As Drusilla stepped through, the door swung shut again, and the room was as it had been moments before.

The secret room, on the other hand, was vastly different. Computer terminals ran the entire length of the far wall, several screens displaying what appeared to be both a series of schematics and co-ordinates along a flight path. Silently, Drusilla slipped herself into the command style chair at the centre of this wall of terminals, and began tapping commands into the console with practiced speed. The central screen changed from a blueprint of the *Odyssey*, to an overview of the Sol System. Several multicoloured dots flashed at various points. There were seven in total. One for each ship. The *Odyssey* was indicated with a red glowing dot, slightly larger than the rest. It had currently left the Sol System, and was approaching its first alien planet, a place that Drusilla knew was desolate. The other ships had fanned out in six other directions. But it was not the ships and their flight plan that she was interested in.

A few more commands later, the view had changed to display a wonderous array of golden clouds. A nebula of sorts which spanned several lightyears, twisted and flowed like water among the stars that surrounded it. A few more taps of the console saw the nebula move to the lower half of the screen, and above it, was nothing.

A large black void filled the screen, visible only as a phenomenon rather than a malfunction because of the few stars bordering it, giving it a definitive edge. The co-ordinates marker on the screen labelled it as 'unknown expanse.' Drusilla rested her face on the palm of her hand, and stared at the co-ordinates. An hour went by, with her not moving from her position, and her eyes never moving from the screen.

After ninety minutes, directly in the middle of the expanse, a locator dot flashed into life. Three flashes, and it was gone again. Drusilla sat back in her chair and her smile grew wide, her eyes gleaming with excitement in the glow of the displays.

"So, there you are."

FOUR

Harry eagerly tapped away at his tablet, putting the finishing touches to the first mission report, which would make up the bulk of their first transmission back to Earth. It had been three weeks so far and as of yet, there had been nothing of interest. Four planets so far had yielded no life, and insufficient minerals and conditions to support human life. Still, the chance to set foot on an alien world that wasn't a part of his own solar system had captivated Harry's attention each time. He had felt like one of Earth's ancient mariners, sailing on the oceans with no idea what they would come across next. The freedom it had presented them, was something that Harry was grasping for now. But it was tainted. The constant threat of Drusilla and her presence had soured the experience thus far. He knew she was nowhere near him or his ship, and yet he felt her presence all around him. She had entered his mind so often, that it was as if part of her lived there, holding him back, and pulling on his strings.

"You know Sir, for someone who was so excited to get under way, you're not exactly showing it."

The voice of his first officer, Commander Kelly Dresden, broke him out of his micro-trance and as he looked up, he saw her leaning on the door frame to his quarters. He hadn't even heard the door chime, such was his focus.

"Trust me Kelly, this means everything to me. I just have... other things on my mind."

Kelly gestured to a nearby chair, looking at Harry for permission, to which he nodded, and she sat.

"You know, Admiral, whatever she said to you, she's not here. There's no way she can control the mission from this distance. This is *your* adventure. The *Odyssey* is *your* ship. Not hers."

Kelly was one of the few people who had seemingly picked up on the tension between Harry and Drusilla, and had seen first hand some of the dismissive comments she had thrown his way during tense arguments or discussions. As First Officer, she had been present at many of those meetings, and had needed to bite her tongue hard on more than one occasion.

"That's just the problem, Kelly. She's always here."

He tapped the side of his head, and while at first slightly confused, Kelly began to understand.

"You can tell me to mind my own business, Sir, but how long have you been seeing her?"

Harry wasn't surprised Kelly had figured it out. She was the highest rated officer across the board in the aptitude tests and military training leading up to this mission. It was the reason he had requested she be posted to him. He had watched her throughout her academy days, and saw something special in her. If he was honest to himself, with his crumbling marriage, if it hadn't been Drusilla, it probably would have been Kelly Dresden.

"A year. Give or take. To be honest Kelly, it's more like I'm not seeing her. I mean she's there, and in the moment I am present physically, but after that, I'm pretty sure she's running the show, and I'm just a bystander."

Nobody onboard the *Odyssey* knew about Drusilla's abilities besides Harry, but given the war on Jupiter with the Darla, there had been rumours surrounding the telepathic abilities of that race in particular. Kelly had not fought on Jupiter, but was present in the aftermath, and she too had heard the stories. It was not beyond the realms of possibility that there were other species with similar talents.

"Harry," she began, placing a hand on his knee and softening her official stance, "don't let her control you. Whatever it is she wants, she'll have to get it herself. Humanity is not her private army."

Trying desperately not to reciprocate Kelly's gesture, Harry smiled and nodded in resignation.

"Yes. We are."

Kelly removed her hand, and her expression turned to one of despair. She hadn't gotten through to him. Either that, or he had been so dominated by Drusilla that he really believed what he was saying. There was no time for further debate, however, as the ship was rocked violently by what felt distinctly like weapons fire. Harry and Kelly exchanged a momentary panicked glance, before leaping to their feet and rushing back to the bridge.

"Report!" demanded Harry.

"Disruptor fire Sir. Unknown origin."

"Helm, full stop. Tactical, shielding to maximum and standby weapons."

"Aye Admiral!"

Commander Dresden slid into her seat at operations, relieving the duty officer there.

"Bringing up the viewscreen now, Admiral," she said.

The large bowed window at the front of the bridge fizzled away from its standard starfield view and gave a live view of directly ahead of them. There was no sign of an attacker.

"Shift to aft view, Commander."

Kelly entered the command and the tip of the rear engines were visible on screen, and out behind the *Odyssey*, a medium sized vessel was banking around, seemingly preparing for a second run.

"Any identification markers?" Harry asked.

"Negative Admiral. Nothing matches any ships in the database. It's not of the Sol System, that much I can tell you."

Kelly was frustrated that despite a wealth of information taken from both Mars and Jupiter during the wars, they had no idea what they were facing. She was always a battle ready warrior, and as the second in command, felt particularly troubled at the lack of knowledge before her. She tried to remind herself that this was part of the deep space experience, but it was hard to break a well drilled habit.

"Tactical, do we have weapons lock?"

"Almost Admiral. We should have confirmed target in fifteen seconds."

Harry nodded and rubbed his chin, the stubble already forming a five-o-clock shadow, despite having shaved just that morning. Must be the stress, he thought.

"As soon as they're in range, target their engines only. I want to find out who the hell they are."

"Aye Sir. Ten seconds."

The tension on the bridge was palpable. The only noise was that of the consoles beeping, and commands being input. Even the alert sirens which echoed throughout the whole ship had gone quiet. The glowing red emergency lights were the only sense that a threat was imminent.

"Five seconds."

Harry felt himself leaning forward in his chair as he saw the ship get ever closer to his own engines. He only hoped they would get their shot off first.

"Three seconds."

Harry noticed there was something familiar about the vessel now he could see it more clearly.

"Two seconds."

There may not have been a match in the database, but somehow, he *knew* that ship.

"One... in range now Sir!"

"FIRE!"

A beam of blue light burst from the rear of the *Odyssey*, and sliced through the darkness of space, leaving a glow across the hull as it struck the enemy vessel's starboard engine. They attempted to break off, but were too slow to react, and despite the majority of the hit being absorbed by their own shielding, the enemy vessel took a direct hit.

"Damage report?"

"Direct hit to their starboard engine, their shields are down to eighty-six percent. They're breaking off, Sir."

"Breaking off?"

"Yes Admiral. Their engines are powering up. Looks like they're gonna make a run for it."

Not on my watch, thought Harry. Nobody attacks the flagship and leaves without an explanation.

"Lay in a pursuit course, Ensign."

"Aye Sir!"

The viewscreen switched back to a fore view, and as Commander Dresden attempted to take as many scans as she could, a bright light burst from the back of the enemy vessel. Briefly dazed by the brightness, it took a moment or two for her to figure out what had happened.

"Oh shit."

Harry looked up and squinted just enough to see the small dark projectile heading directly for them.

"Ensign, evasive manoeuvres!" Harry screamed at his pilot.

But between changing from the previously inputted pursuit course and taking evasive action, too much time elapsed. They weren't gonna get out of the way in time.

"All hands, brace for impact!"

Harry's cries travelled around the entire ship through every speaker on board. The attempt at moving the ship had turned the *Odyssey* to a forty-five degree slanted angle, and when the torpedo finally struck the ship, it broke through the shielding, tore a hole in the hull, and blasted right through to the other side. The impact blew out several consoles on the bridge. The tactical station erupted in a furious display of shattered glass and broken circuitry, sending the officer flying through the air, landing at Harry's feet. Ripple explosions rumbled throughout the ship, and in the areas exposed to space, dozens of soldiers were sucked out into the cold vacuum. Cracks shot along the hull on both the dorsal and ventral sections around the point of impact, before what seemed like hours later, the emergency forcefields sealed off the breaches.

As things began to calm down on the bridge, Harry's eyes were still transfixed on the young man laying at his feet. His eyes were wide open, one of which was white and glazed over. The right side of his face was gone, bone clearly visible amongst the charred flesh. The hair on that side had been all but vapourised and blood coated both the soldier's uniform, and the deck plate on which he now lay.

It was only Kelly Dresden's voice which brought him back to the moment.

"Admiral," she said, gesturing at the viewscreen. "They're gone."

FIVE

Seventeen crew members were dead or missing. A cascade effect in the power systems had rendered the star drive offline, leaving them with minimal impulse power, and intermittent thrusters for manoeuvring. However, Harry Ransome was not dismayed or preoccupied with his perceived control by Drusilla any longer. No. Now he was pissed off. And the conference room knew it.

"I want to know who the fuck just tore a hole through my ship like tissue paper and then boogeyed on out without any more than a light scratch!"

He slammed his fist on the glass table, and the scattered information tablets on the surface jumped in response. Kelly was trying to make sense of the scans she had taken, but as of yet, she could identify no vital systems that could make viable targets should they meet again. They had managed to capture several images of the vessel itself, some of them containing a high level of detail. The ship itself was almost pearlescent. It appeared black, camouflaging against the stars, but when it turned to bank, it shimmered a dark green. The vessel was shaped like an arrowhead, pointed at the front, and sweeping back into two similar points at the rear either side. Below each rear point, was a rectangular engine exhaust, and below the main body of the ship, central to the craft, was a series of disruptor cannons, mounted so closely to the hull that they would not impact the slipstream ability of the vessel at high speed. She was a hunter.

"I've managed to analyse the torpedo they hit us with, there were several fragments embedded in the hull around the affected areas on Deck Eight," Kelly offered. "But you're not gonna like it Admiral."

Harry gradually lowered himself into his seat, allowing the other officers around him to breathe a little easier.

"I already don't like it Commander. We've barely been out here a month, and the damage we have sustained may force us to turn back. We were attacked without provocation, by what at this point, seems like pirates. So tell me, what have you found out about this torpedo?"

Kelly took a deep breath.

"It's transphasic."

A few gasps around the room from two of the engineers, who sported visible injuries themselves from being thrown around during the attack.

"Are you certain?" Harry asked in a hushed breath.

Kelly simply nodded.

Harry stood up and walked over to the window, gazing out at the stars, but not paying them any attention. A transphasic weapon, on Earth, was experimental and they did not have the technology to create even a concept or prototype. Once fired, it had the ability to transform its molecular structure, allowing it to theoretically pass through any shielding or hull material, before detonating *after* the point of impact causing maximum damage. In short, it moved through the ship and detonated once inside.

"That would explain the damage to the *Odyssey*," volunteered one of the engineers. "A clean hole, right through, and a spread pattern of collateral damage. It's consistent with an internal explosion."

Kelly nodded, and brought up an artistic rendition of what the weapon looked like prior to detonation. But Harry wasn't interested. He was still troubled by the familiarity of the ship. It had to be something he had seen in Drusilla's mind when the two had shared a telepathic link. He had never laid eyes on a ship like that before, but still, he *knew* it.

"Estimated time to complete minimum repairs before we head home?" he asked, finally turning away from the window.

"Actually, Admiral, I don't think we need to head home," replied Kelly.

"But the damage is..."

"Severe, yes. But most of it is structural. In terms of functionality, star drive power should be back up and running in nine hours, bulkheads have already been sealed on Decks Five through Seven, and any critical systems can be bypassed. I don't see why we cannot complete the repairs on the move."

That is why Harry Ransome had chosen Kelly Dresden. He even felt a small smile spread across his face. He wasn't sure how she had managed it, but if he could continue the mission without turning around, then that was his preferred option. He nodded enthusiastically, the smile growing wider.

"If you can get us ship-shape again Commander without turning this boat around, then get it done."

Kelly smiled in return.

"Yes Admiral!"

"Dismissed."

Everyone got up from their chairs and headed for the door, a newfound resilience forming in their minds. Harry held up a hand.

"Oh and Commander?"

Kelly stopped and turned.

"Yes Admiral?"

"Get those weapons increased. We're going to hunt those bastards down."

SIX

Drusilla read the report for the third time. It was the first transmission to be sent from the *Odyssey* and as she finished the document once again, she felt the anger rising within her.

"Lying human cunt!"

Over a month into deep space exploration on a mission she had authorised, and put into motion, to hunt down the Darla renegades, and Harry Ransome was reporting nothing of any significance. She knew that to be a lie. If they had followed the flight plan that she had given them, and that she had been tracking, then they would already have reached a settlement of the Darla. She knew it existed, but she could not be seen to be the one behind the attack. No, her vengeance must come from the darkness, behind the scenes. She would not risk her species being identified, and a Darla warship sent to her homeworld. She had kept them safe for this long, she would not take risks now.

But the time had come for action. The human admiral was not keeping to his end of the bargain. She knew as soon as she cut the tether with his mind that there was a chance he would run. This is why humanity was better off being part of an experiment, she thought. Give them free will and they fritter about the galaxy like knotweed, infesting everywhere, devastating more than they create, and then vanish onto the next target. It was part of the reason they were in the mess they were now. Earth was dying. She knew it. The humans knew it. But the denial was immense. Life was continuing on Earth almost as normal. And yet there was no accountability for what these hairless apes were doing to their own home. Typical ignorance, she feared, would lead to them trying to reach out among the stars for someone else to fix their problems. But Drusilla knew that would never happen. She had after all, made sure of it.

As the deserts enlarged and reclaimed Las Vegas, and most of Northern Africa, the tides were also rising. They had around a decade of time remaining before it really was too late. But Drusilla decided to give Ransome one more month. She knew that their current course would take them near a trading station and that at that point they would need to dock for maintenance. The human ships were strong and built to last, thanks to Drusilla's nudges in the right direction. But being on the move for eight to ten weeks would force them to stop. This was the home of a known associate of Drusilla's. He was a former neighbour of sorts, in that he was from a species on a neighbouring planet to her own. Being over nine hundred years old had its advantages for him. His client list was extensive, and Drusilla had last seen him when she bartered passage to Earth. She had contacted him in advance to instruct the man to introduce himself to the crew of the *Odyssey*. He was to tell them the story he and Drusilla had created. The story designed to lure humanity to the brink. Toward their only useful purpose.

She knew once this tale was transmitted back to Earth in the monthly report, word would spread, more ships would be built, and humanity would burst forth into the stars toward their fate. Earth was inconsequential to her. It was within her power to save it, but she had no desire to do so. It would serve as a military outpost whether it was lush and vibrant with life, or a desert moon. All she needed was humanity to vacate the lot.

One more month.

She glanced out of her window, and admired the recently completed starship *Northwestern*. She was a smaller vessel than the *Odyssey* and her peers, but was designed for speed and rescue rather than transportation of colonists. It was her backup escape plan. There was a vessel on each of the three human colonies. One month. If she had not heard the expected details from Harry Ransome within one month, then she was taking the *Northwestern*, and hunting him down.

SEVEN

"Scans coming in now, Sir."

The image on the viewscreen was that of a large man-made rock floating through space. Constructed from metal alloys, many of which were unfamiliar to humans, the structure was designed to appear at least to the naked eye as a devastated asteroid. Admiral Ransome was unsure as to whether their scanning equipment was simply too advanced for that disguise to work, or the design itself had purpose. No ship coming near to the facility would mistake it for actual geological material.

"It's definitely a large facility Admiral," reported the Science Lieutenant. "I'm reading several eateries, eighteen docking ports, moderate shields, substantial weaponry, and what appears to be a large medical facility on one of the lower levels."

At this point, the doors opened at the rear of the bridge and Commander Dresden joined Harry at his side.

"Interesting design," she noted, having caught the tail end of the Lieutenant's summary. "Wonder if they're friendly."

Harry nodded, his arms folded, thumb stroking his beard, which he had noted was now substantially more peppered with whites and greys than when he had left Earth two months prior.

"Well I don't think we have much choice but to find out. We need supplies after the attack from our mystery friends, and after two months, I expect there's a few people who would like to stretch their legs somewhere that wasn't the *Odyssey*."

Kelly was definitely one of them. She had frequented the gym so often since they left home, that she had almost worn one of the rowing machines out already. And since the attack, the swimming pool was still out of commission, thanks in no small part to the bottom having been blasted into space. Harry nodded at her, and she took a rigid stance next to her commanding officer.

"Commander Teale, open a channel to the facility," she ordered. Harry had been trying to give her more authority over the mission since the attack, in order to prepare her for eventual command. What she didn't know that Harry did, was that whenever this mission concluded, he would be promoting her to Captain, and handing the *Odyssey* over to her. He stood back and allowed her to continue.

"Channel open, Commander."

Kelly cleared her throat.

"This is Commander Kelly Dresden of the human vessel *Odyssey*. Please respond."

The bridge fell silent, with the quiet punctuated by the odd bleep or tone from a console or two. It seemed as though they were about to be ignored, but as Kelly opened her mouth to repeat the hail, the viewscreen switched to an image of a very large and very green skinned individual. The hair on the person's head had been shaved on both sides to the scalp, leaving a flared mohawk of jet black in the centre. His eyes glowed yellow, but were similar in appearance to their own, and his clothing was similar to that of an

Earth blacksmith. Despite the initial fuzzy picture, the muscles on the man were easily definable. He was easily seven feet in height and Kelly suspected at least four feet wide.

"Humans, huh?" growled the alien. "Well I suppose you had to figure out how to fly eventually."

The familiarity with their species caught both Kelly and Harry off guard, but continuing to lead the inquiry, Kelly probed further.

"I'm afraid you have us at a disadvantage Mister...?"

"Gryffin. Tolian Gryffin. I'm the Station Master here. I suspect, Commander, that you are in need of maintenance, or else why would you have hailed our facility?"

Guy really cuts through the bullshit, Kelly thought.

"We are indeed, if you are willing to accommodate us Mr Gryffin? We are still lacking a few vital components to complete our repairs following an attack several weeks ago."

That caught his attention, and his posture noticeable shifted. He even managed a small smile.

"Attack you say? Well there's no point in making more enemies through refusal, I guess. We shall see what we can do. Please bring your vessel around to Docking Port Seven. I will have a team meet you there, and your crew will be free to disembark."

A surge of satisfaction rose through Kelly's chest. Her first encounter with an alien species outside the Sol System, and it had been an immediate success. But then that happiness began to be pushed back down by the impending dread of one sentence running through her mind.

That was too easy.

This time, Harry decided to step forward and address Tolian Gryffin.

"Station Master, I don't see any docking ports. Perhaps you can direct us?"

Gryffin examined Harry's face for a moment, before replying.

"You will Admiral Ransome."

The screen returned to the exterior view, and the entire image of the rock structure rippled momentarily, until a cloaking shield which must have been disguising the facility dropped, and a space station three times the size of the initial structure shimmered into existence.

"Woah!" exclaimed Teale at the communications station. "Bigger on the outside. How 'bout that."

The docking ports were now clearly visible with their large numbered markings on the bay doors, and Kelly indicated for the pilot to head for door seven. As they approached, they cut main engines, and switched to thrusters.

"Certainly impressive, Admiral, wouldn't you say?" asked Kelly.

Harry nodded.

"Indeed Commander, and you did exceptionally well in securing our docking here."

"Thank you Sir."

"There's just one question I don't understand."

Kelly looked puzzled.

"And what would that be Admiral?"

Harry turned his head so that his mouth was inches from Kelly's left ear. He whispered so nobody else would hear him.

"How did he know my name?"

EIGHT

The smile faded from Tolian Gryffin's face immediately. He was unfamiliar with the human profanity, but the tone of its delivery told him all he needed to know. Admiral Harry Ransome was calling him a liar.

"You should be careful Admiral. You're not amongst friends now. And you're a long way from home. If you choose to question someone's honour, you should be prepared to test that notion."

Harry downed his third glass of something the bartender had called Monster Blood, and grimaced at the strength behind it, before looking Gryffin right in the eyes.

"You're telling me, that there is some magical and mystical phenomenon on the edge of known space that can somehow transport anyone who enters it, back through time? And not only that, but it has the god-like ability to figure out when you were happiest in your lifetime, and dump you out of said time travel at just the right moment? I think you've been drinking too much of this 'whatever-the-fuck' it's called, my large green friend."

Harry motioned to stand, but the effects of the alcohol forced him to appear to change his mind, and sit back down again. Not wishing to appear foolish, he attempted to continue the conversation.

"And just how exactly do you know about this?"

Gryffin saw that he had, through one method or another, gained at least a small percentage of Harry's attention. Now it was time for the hard sell.

"I know, because I've been there."

Harry made a dismissive gesture, but Gryffin saw there was something in his eyes that betrayed his true feelings. He needed to know more. Whether he would use that to ultimately dismiss the idea, or use it to convince himself to embrace it, only time would tell.

"But you're still here."

Gryffin nodded.

"It may surprise you to know Admiral, but I am the happiest I have ever been, right here, running all of this."

He gestured around him at the corroding pipework, groaning doors and filthy floors of the bar they were currently sat in.

"Here? In this, and forgive me for being so blunt but, shithole?"

Gryffin laughed a hearty belly laugh.

"You think this is a shithole? My friend you have *no* idea."

Although the line was delivered in a jocular fashion, those last four words were tinged with menace. Harry felt as though Gryffin had essentially told him to fuck around and find out. He decided while he focused on overcoming the effects of the Monster Blood liquor, he would try and absorb whatever notions Gryffin was about to bestow on him.

"I travelled there with a small crew. There were nine of us altogether. We had heard the rumours, but I, like you, was dismissive. For me, it was more a scouting mission for raw materials, and anything new we may find in the area. At that point, the Saraswathi System was practically uncharted. But there it was. A huge great red and violet energy nebula. We travelled along its outer edge for two days and still failed to make it to the centre of its perimeter. There were no signs of anything we could scavenge, and no nearby moons or planets to trade with. What there were, however, were incredibly high levels of tachyons."

Now that was a word that captured Harry's attention. Tachyons only meant one thing, and until this very moment, they were deemed to be theoretical.

"Tachyons... as in..."

"Time travel, Admiral, yes."

Harry blew out his cheeks but despite the new information, he remained sceptical. However, that scepticism was not as deep rooted as it had been at the start of this conversation.

"But you're still here, which means you didn't go in. So how do you know the rumours were true?"

Gryffin downed his own glass of liquor, and gestured for another from the barman.

"There was a man among my crew who had encountered a species at our previous port of repairs. I believe you may have heard of them. Darla."

Harry felt every fibre of his being sober up instantaneously. He knew the Darla alright. And boy did they know him.

"I see I am correct. My crewman spent the night in a bar very much like this, discussing this Horizon phenomenon with the Darla male. He was the one who insisted we explore it at once. I suspected that there had been some kind fo mental manipulation from this Darla, because this man who I had served with for almost a decade, was not one to make rash decisions. In the space of a few hours, his personality was mutated into some kind of desperate creature.

When we reached the Horizon, and I refused to enter, he shot three of my crew, drove a blade through my stomach, and launched an escape pod into the Horizon."

Harry glanced down to where Gryffin's hand was stroking a large scar on his abdomen, visible through a gap in the material.

"Your man, did you ever see him again?"

Gryffin smiled and nodded as the bartender brought over another two glasses.

"He's pouring your next drink."

Harry stopped reaching towards the glass, and looked up at the bartender who was now smiling at him, taking some sort of perverse pleasure in pulling the surprise on the human Admiral.

"Pleasure to meet you Admiral," spoke the bartender. "My name is Sunyi Kamen."

Harry was unsure of where to look. Clearly the bartender was not living what Harry would call his happiest moment. How could he be? He felt as though this was a hugely elaborate hoax and he was the punchline of a joke. Hazing for the new species in town. But Gryffin's voice lowered and the smiles faded.

"You see Admiral, Sunyi here went into the Horizon. He found himself twenty years earlier, standing at the bedside of his no longer deceased wife, precisely five minutes after the birth of their daughter. He had returned to his happiest moment. And now, twenty years later, he found me and told me all about it."

"And his family?"

"Living happily on a nearby ocean moon. Sunyi takes the transport home to them every night. So you see Admiral, the Horizon is real. It allowed Sunyi here to save his wife and child from their brutal murder at the hands of thieves a decade ago. An event which he had previously been off-world for. Now what would you do with a power like that, hmm?"

Harry felt as though his brain was going to melt. This was impossible. There was no way that anything like this could exist, let alone have provided him with a living breathing example. No, this was still feeling like a cruel joke to him. But it did force him to think long and hard about when he had indeed been at his happiest. Could he even remember it? So much pain and strife and war had burned through his fairly short lifetime. But then he thought of her. The day Harry met his wife for the first time. Annette had been assigned to escort Harry around the opening of the new shipyard in southern Spain. Ultimately, of course, this would be the very place which constructed the *Odyssey*, but back then it was to be used for smaller, interstellar craft to ferry supplies to and from the colonies on both Mars and Jupiter. He had fallen for her immediately. Her laid back approach to the rules, telling him shortcuts to get around the red tape of getting decisions made. She knew a considerable amount of information for someone who was merely a low level clerical officer. That was the moment that he knew, should this Horizon exist, and he were to enter it, that he would find himself at once more.

But he couldn't indulge it. He had seen too much, learned too much and experienced the harsh truth of reality to lose himself in fantasy. There was already too much at stake. It wouldn't help him save the Earth. Even when he and Annette first met, the planet was already doomed, it had simply started more slowly than the rate it was currently decaying. There was far more at stake, and he couldn't afford to deviate from his plan. Find a new home for his people, track down his attackers, and get as far away from Drusilla as possible.

"I'm sorry Mr Gryffin, but I just don't believe such a place can exist. Thank you for your hospitality, and I bid you a good day."

Gryffin did not appear disappointed as Harry approached the

entrance to the bar. In fact, he was rather pleased with how the conversation had gone. Harry, suddenly remembered through the fog of the alcohol and the sensational conversation he had just had, that there was one unfinished piece of business.

"Mr Gryffin, how did you know my name?"

Gryffin stood and towered over his apparent time-travelling barman, and glared intensely at Harry.

"I believe we have a mutual friend."

Harry did not need to ask any further details. He knew who this mutual friend was. And he suspected she had a long mane of blue hair. That was all he needed to move his legs forward. His mind was set. Finish the repairs, gather the supplies, and get the fuck away from this place as fast as the star drive would carry them.

Moments after Harry exited the bar, Gryffin did the same. Having watched her commanding officer and his new associate throughout their conversation, Kelly thought she would be erring on the side of the Admiral. The side of logic. The side of common sense. And yet her thoughts drifted back to those of her father. Killed during the first offensive on Mars. She thought back to the week before when she had revealed to him that she had been accepted into the academy and how proud he was of her. The weekend that they spent together training alone in the forests of Yellowstone national park. That was the happiest time of her life. She could change his mind about leaving for Mars. She was the one who had ushered him out the door when he was reluctant to go. And he had never come back. But this time, this time would be different. And with that thought in mind, Commander Kelly Dresden stood up from the booth in the dark corner of the bar, and headed over towards Sunyi.

"Another round Miss?" he enquired.

Kelly shook her head.

"Tell me everything you know about this Horizon."

Just outside the entrance of the bar, Tolian Gryffin glanced back inside at the Commander, and smiled.

"Mission accomplished."

NINE

Considering the fact that she had travelled through space literally dozens of times in her life, Drusilla was still uncomfortable at high speeds. The low rumbling of the engines travelled throughout her entire body, despite her being the only one to experience it. The heightened brain development needed for telepathy, was showing one of its few downsides. Much of her fury had subsided since the delivery of Admiral Ransome's second report. Despite her conversations over subspace communication with Tolian Gryffin, not one word of the meeting was mentioned in the second transmission. Simply more words of finding empty planets and barren moons.

She had wasted no time in preparing the *Northwestern* for departure, but the lack of available crew had meant it was almost three and a half months since the fleet had left Earth. The third report from the *Odyssey* had not arrived. Drusilla suspected the effects of Gryffin and his tales of wonder had started affecting the crew. While this had always been the plan, Drusilla had figured she'd have longer. After all, the primary mission was the Darla and their extinction. Humanity would only move to its main purpose afterwards. Well, those who were left.

The *Northwestern* had continued being developed after its completion. While originally being constructed with the same materials, engines and resources as the rest of the Utopia fleet, the *Northwestern* had remained in development. The engines on this ship, therefore, were faster than those of the *Odyssey*. The estimated time to intercept Harry Ransome was somewhere in the region of six weeks, following their longer than planned stop at Grabthor Beta. Drusilla planned a stop there herself. She planned to have a word with Tolian Gryffin about bringing in one of his employees to enhance the little story they concocted. It may have been the element which tipped the plans into motion too soon. But as with most things in her life, only time would tell.

She had ordered that transmissions be sent back to Earth in the same vein as the rest of the Utopia ships. One per month on the anniversary of launch. She had also ordered that those messages be of the exact information sent by the *Odyssey*. No point in panicking the lab rats. They needed accurate results, not skewed and flawed products. She was relieved that nobody seemed concerned with the other vessels in the fleet, and everyone was focussing on the disappearance of the *Odyssey*. It would keep attention away from the *real* destination of the other six ships for a while longer. Not that anyone on Earth would ever find them.

Little did Drusilla know, that she would not catch up to Harry Ransome in six weeks time. The problem with being so dominant and convinced of your iron grip on a situation, is that invariably, at some point and like most things in life, it all goes to shit. However powerful she was, and however many friends she had in high places, or the strength of her persuasive telepathic powers, she could not control *everything* in the galaxy.

And it was due to that incontrovertible fact, that President of Earth, Drusilla, would not see the face of Admiral Harry Ransome for almost ten years.

TEN

THE SITUATION onboard the *Odyssey* was now reaching fever pitch. There had been more than a dozen fights break out amongst the crew since leaving Grabthor Beta, and the brig was now in constant use. And it was here, in the briefing room, that he found himself unsure of what to say to the cause of the problems. It was a situation that he never felt he would be in, and therefore had no idea how to deal with it.

"Of all the people to cause mistrust and unruliness onboard this ship, I never thought it would be you Kelly."

Harry's words were tinged with disappointment and hurt. Kelly Dresden was the one person he trusted more than anyone. For her to attempt to incite some kind of insurrection against him was unfathomable.

"I'm sorry Harry, I didn't mean for it to go this far," she replied. Her facial expressions seemed sincere. She was aware of the consequences her words had had on the crew, and she had seen for herself the chaos unfolding, particularly in the lower decks of the ship.

"What I don't understand, is how someone as intelligent as you can even contemplate the existence of such a place, let alone try and convince others of the fact."

Kelly's shoulders slumped, and she shook her head. Neither did she, in truth. One moment she had been enjoying a beer, or as close to it as she could find on that godforsaken lump of a station, and the next it was as if someone had whispered something in her ear. She had felt compelled to investigate, beyond her own interests. She couldn't explain it.

"The best way I can describe the situation Admiral, is that... it wasn't me."

While Kelly expected to be ridiculed for such a statement, the exact opposite happened. Harry's eyes widened, and his own demeanour shifted to one of extreme discomfort. Wasting no time, he gestured for the two security guards flanking Kelly to be dismissed, and gestured for her to follow him. Confused but relieved, Kelly followed Harry onto the bridge and she stood at his side as he sat down in his chair.

"Computer, locate President Drusilla."

The command caused several sets of eyes to lock on him in confusion, but Harry paid them no mind.

"President Drusilla is not aboard the Odyssey."

So it wasn't her. But someone was responsible.

"Commander Teale, are there any communications being directed at this ship right now? On any wavelength or bandwidth?"

Thinking her commanding officer had perhaps enjoyed too many glasses of Monster Blood on the station, she expected to find nothing, but when her own eyes widened in surprise, and she turned back to Harry, he knew he'd been right.

"Yes Admiral. I'm picking up a very low frequency transmission. It appears to be coming from six-hundred kilometres off our starboard bow. It's directed at... at the bridge, Sir."

A smile crept into the corner of Harry's face as he directed Kelly to take her post.

"Something tells me Commander, that you weren't to blame after all."

Still a blend of confusion and relief, Kelly nodded and slid behind her console.

"Tactical, scan for any movement on the starboard side that looks out of place. I'm looking for a cloaked ship or one with some kind of dampening field."

"Aye Sir."

The two tactical officers, Clarkson and Perry, immediately began running through the various sensor arrays on the ship each scanning for a different form of disguise. Engine trails, reflective panelling, energy signatures, anything.

"Helm, full stop."

"Now reading full stop, Sir."

Harry leaned forward in his chair, elbow poised on his right knee, waiting and staring at the viewscreen. He had been in far too many firefights in the cosmos to be caught out here. Somebody was out there. They were watching the *Odyssey*, and now the ball was firmly in their court.

"Come out, come out, wherever you are…" he sang under his breath.

His eyes were so focussed on the stars on the viewscreen that after a short while, several of them rippled as if a stone had been thrown into a great lake.

"THERE!" he shouted.

Without a moment of hesitation, the tactical team redirected targeting sensors to the spot indicated by the Admiral.

"Ready Sir!"

"FIRE!"

Both fore disrupter cannons erupted with blue light as beams of energy burst forth toward the disruption and with a single hit, their cloaking shield was disabled, revealing the vessel to be the very same one which had attacked them months earlier.

"Direct hit Admiral," reported Clarkson. "Their cloak is down, and shields are down to seventy-two percent."

"Nice shooting Mr Clarkson. Now let's see if we can get that percentage down a little more, shall we?"

Clarkson smiled, and nodded. He handed weapons control over to Ensign Perry who utilised short bursts of weapons fire to target specific subsystems. Two shots to each engine and the white hot glow as they tried to flee once more, went out like a doused candle. Three more and their thrusters were gone too.

"Systems show all propulsion disabled and shields down to seventeen percent, Admiral."

Harry grinned and stood from his chair.

"Good work tactical. Commander Dresden, lifesigns?"

Kelly scanned the ship now floating aimlessly before them. But her readings were not consistent. In fact they were downright confusing.

"Affirmative Admiral, but... I don't understand the readings I'm getting back."

Harry stepped down to stand behind her and glance at her console. He understood her confusion. The readout claimed there were fifteen lifesigns on board the ship. Then the next moment, they were gone. Then they reappeared but were only showing five. The process repeated ten times, each time displaying a different number of lifesigns.

Harry looked at the ship. He still couldn't understand why he recognised the configuration. And then it hit him.

"Commander Teale, what kind of signal was the transmission?"

"A low frequency signal with a steady pattern, Sir."

"And can you pinpoint exactly where on the bridge it was being directed?"

Teale never got to reply to Harry's question. The disruptor strike hit her in the left shoulder sending her careering to the floor, crying in agony. Before Harry could turn around, six more shots had taken out multiple crew members including both tactical officers. As Harry finally turned around to face the source of the shots, Kelly turned the weapon towards him. Her eyes were glazed over with a milky film of white. But things got immediately worse, as on the viewscreen behind her, five more ships decloaked alongside the disabled vessel and they took up an attack posture. Harry sighed and gritted his teeth with anger.

"The Darla."

ELEVEN

THREE WEEKS HAD GONE by since the capture of the *Odyssey* and her crew. Three weeks of beatings, torturous mind probes and travelling in a direction very far from their planned flight path. Kelly winced as one of the Darla medics cleaned up her latest head wound.

"Keep still human, or you'll end up with more than a gash to the forehead," barked the medic.

"Anyone ever tell you that you have a lousy fucking bedside manner?"

Kelly groaned in agony, as a nearby guard sent a searing pain into Kelly's mind, causing her to drop to her knees off the medical bed, grabbing furiously at her temples.

"Leave her alone!"

The laboured and groggy voice caught the attention of the guard, and he ceased his mental torture. Kelly dropped to the floor unconscious, the pain simply too much to bear. The medics lifted her back onto the bed and treated her wounds.

"I thought you'd be dead by now," the guard spoke through gritted teeth. "I see you human puppets are tougher than you look. That's what she must see in you."

Harry Ransome looked like a completely different man. Large chunks of his face were swollen, blackened and either bleeding or weeping. His formerly grey beard was now stained red with his own blood, and considerably longer. His hair was wild, and also had streaks of crimson running through it, and his uniform had been all but shredded, several gashes and wounds visible on his chest and abdomen. He could barely stand, and was being propped up by two other guards.

"Sorry to disappoint you," Harry spat in reply.

The guard took a stride toward him, and gripped his chin in his hand, yanking Harry's eyes upward to look at him directly.

"Tell us what she wants from you, or we'll kill your crew one by one. I think I'll start with this loud mouth female. Yes. I think I'll enjoy tearing her mind apart."

He licked his lips, trying to get a rise out of Harry, and had he been even an ounce stronger in that moment, he would have done. But the beating he had taken was too much, and he slumped forward.

"A pity. Get him fixed up, and send him back to his cell. We can try again later."

The office of the Darla Captain was not too dissimilar to his own. It was enough to make Harry wonder if Drusilla had simply stolen their ship design and copied it over to the Utopia fleet, making minor changes. It would certainly explain how she knew so much about ship design without ever having built one. The Captain himself, a man called Darven, was pouring a cup of green tea, the steam rising with the liquid level in the glass receptacle.

"I would offer you some Admiral, but it is deadly to humans, and I still need information from you."

Harry coughed at the scent of the tea filling his lungs like smoke.

"I've told you everything I know," he replied through laboured breaths.

"Hmm."

Darven took a sip of the tea, Harry wincing at the thought that it had not even cooled, and yet Darven showed no discomfort. He lowered the cup and placed both hands on his desk.

"Admiral Ransome, we know a great many things about your friend Drusilla. But how much do you know, hmm?"

That was a question for which Harry couldn't truly offer an honest answer. So he gave the only one he could.

"I feel like I only know what she wants me to know."

Darven nodded.

"An astute summary, Sir. Are you aware that she lost her father during an unfortunate skirmish as a child?"

Harry nodded.

"And are you aware that not only did she blame us for this indiscretion, but she opted to seek revenge on our people?"

Again Harry nodded.

"Then she was more forthcoming with you than she was with her last concubine."

"Her what?"

Darven chuckled to himself.

"You don't honestly think you're the first species she has tried to enslave do you?"

Harry's mind was now swimming. Enslave? Drusilla had promised them a new home, a brighter future. Harry was the only one who knew that she wanted to use the military to hunt the Darla. But enslave *all* humans? No. Apparently reading his mind, Darven interrupted.

"Oh I'm afraid so, Admiral. Drusilla is from a species called the Shran. Much like us, she has telepathic abilities and much like us, she is able to manipulate others into doing her bidding. However, unlike us, she can transmit such thoughts across vast distances. And unlike us, she was never meant to leave her home planet."

Harry's head was pounding from the constant barrage of attacks and healing and attacks and more healing. The cycle had broken his mind, but he was desperately trying to cling on to what Darven was saying as he continued.

"You see, the Shran were once the dominant force across an entire solar system. They ruled with an iron fist, as I believe you humans say. They beat down anybody who stood in their way, and took all the resources from any planet they chose for their own wealth and gain. They sent twelve populated worlds into ruin and poverty. On a scouting mission from our home on Jupiter before we encountered you, one of our military vessels followed a shipment of weapons back to the Shran homeworld. When we became aware of the genocide and evil spreading through that system, we knew we could not simply sit back and do nothing.

And so we acted. We gathered all of our forces, and we fought the Shran for over sixty years. Eventually, we convinced the people of those twelve worlds to rise up with us, and we drove the Shran back to their home world. They were sentenced to remain on their planet forever more, and we took every ounce of technology from them. Their leaders were dead, and it was only the regular folk who remained. A beacon was put in place to warn other species to stay away from the Shran. And that peace lasted for a very long time. And we returned home."

Darven's eyes then grew wistful. Sadness crept across his face, and Harry felt he knew where the story was going next.

"And then *she* came. The elders had told the children nothing of the war, trying to forget such pain and the horrors they had imposed on others. Our chance encounter with Drusilla was mere coincidence. A simple trade mission with one of the newly reinvigorated worlds in their system went wrong, and one of our shuttles crashed on the Shran homeworld. One of the locals ran at the security officer with a pitchfork. Already wounded and panicked from the crash, he fired in self defence. Of course that man turned out to be Drusilla's father. We rescued our crew and fled home, fearful of the impact our interference would have.

Somehow she managed to barter her way off the planet by way of a passing conman by the name of Tolian Gryffin."

Harry's suspicions had been right all along. The whole thing had been a hoax. And half of his crew had fallen for it. Darven saw the change in Harry's expression.

"I take it you have met Mr Gryffin Admiral?"

Harry nodded.

"He's the reason half my crew are fighting amongst themselves to reach some fabled magic doorway into the past."

Darven held up a single finger.

"Ah, my dear Admiral, no. The Horizon may not be an actual route to the past, but it does exist. And so does the Expanse."

"The Expanse?"

Darven nodded.

"An area of space devoid of any life. No stars, no planets, no life, no light. A void in the cosmos stretching an area that would take almost thirty days to cross. An area you do not wish to find yourself in, Admiral."

Harry had been unfortunate enough to venture into a small void at the edge of the Sol System once. It was only thirty-thousand kilometres across, but the absence of light and stars had a severe effect on his mental health in the short time his vessel was trapped there. He shuddered at the thought of another void so large. Darven continued.

"Once freed by Gryffin, Drusilla attempted to coerce another humanoid species into fighting for her. The Titans were a race of ancient warriors, bred for war and conquest. They were each over two thousand years old, and their minds had become weakened by time. They were an ideal target for her. They came in their numbers to Jupiter and war raged on my homeworld. Fortunately, the Titans were too old to sustain heavy battle any longer, and we were able to defeat them and drive them back from our solar system. Drusilla was once again banished to her homeworld.

I had no idea how she escaped a second time, Admiral, but we did not see her again for almost two centuries, and when we did, she was accompanied by humanity. We lost our home, most of our people, and were scattered among the stars. Refugees of the cosmos. Because of *you*."

Darven's storytelling was over. The rage now trembling in his throat as he spoke, and stood from behind the desk.

"You helped her destroy our people. You helped that witch murder us in our beds. You, Admiral, murdered our children. And now she wants you to finish the job. Hah! Drusilla doesn't know where you are, but her endgame for your people was always the same. And so, allow us the honour of sending you on your way ourselves."

A whirring noise began coming from the wall alongside Harry's chair, and as the mechanical blinds raised, the room was bathed in a golden light. The sight was incredible. They appeared to be inside a nebula of some sort, but the strands of energy were like cotton, simply swaying in an imaginary breeze. The colours were so vibrant, in any other scenario it would have brought a tear to Harry's eyes.

And hovering just ahead of the nearest dust cloud, was the *Odyssey*. She was adrift, but seemingly undamaged.

"You will all return to your ship, Admiral. And we will send you to your final destination. Consider it your punishment. You will end your days in the Expanse."

Harry glared at him.

"And what makes you think we won't just fly back out, and hunt you down?" he sneered.

Darven's grin spread wide across his face.

"Just because you can't see anything in the Expanse Admiral, doesn't mean it's empty."

Harry's blood ran cold, as he was lifted from the chair and dragged out of Darven's office. Once the doors were closed, Darven sat down once more, and moved to pour himself another cup of tea. A sharp pain shot through his temple, and he dropped the glass cup on the floor, where it shattered into millions of tiny crystals.

"Come to us...."

The voice echoed around inside Darven's mind. He tried to shake it off, but it came again.

"Come to us..."

"No, it's not... not possible..."

"Come to us..."

Darven's mind glazed over, as did his eyes. He could feel his own consciousness being pushed back into the recesses of his mind, as if someone had taken the wheel. He could see what he was doing, but had no control over it. Moments later, the *Odyssey* began to move towards the edge of the Saraswathi Nebula. A comms alert beeped from Darven's communicator.

"Captain, the *Odyssey* autopilot has been engaged. She is headed into the Expanse."

Darven's head twitched left to right, before a voice that did not belong to him replied to his navigation officer.

"Follow them in."

A confused Ensign on the other end of the channel was unsure he had heard correctly.

"Excuse me Sir?"

The creature now possessing Darven's body smiled.

"You heard me. Follow them in."

TWELVE

The grogginess caught Harry by surprise. It almost took a few moments for him to register that he hadn't passed out. Everything swirled around him, and it felt as if he was on a ship on the ocean, cascading between rolling waves. And then it passed. There was just enough time for him to become fully cognitive before the *Odyssey* lost all power. Everything. The moment the ship crossed the threshold of the Expanse, every system on the ship went into standby. Luckily, moments later, the emergency reserves kicked in, ensuring a continued stream of life support throughout the ship.

Darven and his crew had locked in a course using thrusters only and sent them on their way. Harry was still unsure as to the nature of this supposed demise, but already the added darkness seemed to envelop him. A cold sweat began to form on his brow as he looked around the bridge at his other officers, who unlike him, *had* been rendered unconscious.

Kelly came to first, and unsure of where she was, fell out of her chair and faceplanted the floor.

"Mother fucker!" she screamed, the noise seeming to echo throughout the ship.

As she struggled to her feet, Harry could see a thin trickle of blood coming down from just above her left eyebrow.

"Kelly, you okay?" he asked, his voice still hoarse.

She shot him a look of pure rage.

"Okay? You wanna know if I'm fucking okay Harry? What do you think?! Why don't we try letting some mind reader control you like a fucking puppet and see how you like it!"

Several quick and sharp breaths followed her outburst, and she was struggling to maintain any form of calm or composure. Harry staggered over to her, and placed his hands on her shoulders to steady her.

"Come on Kelly, breathe. Take slower and deeper breaths, I need you focused, come on now."

After a few minutes, Kelly managed to calm herself enough to talk, and nodded to Harry that she was okay. Around them, several others began to wake up, and after explaining to them where they were and the things that Darven had said, he attempted to come up with a plan.

"We need to restore main power, and crack whatever security measures they put in place for the engines. Our priority is getting out of this expanse as soon as possible."

Commander Teale, now sporting a sling on her injured arm from a possessed Kelly's earlier shooting, stepped forward.

"Admiral, what exactly is the expanse? Why would they send us here?"

Before Harry could answer, there was a bloodcurdling scream from somewhere beyond the bridge. Nobody dared move, too afraid of what they might find. The cries of agony increased and turned to gargling noises before being cut off abruptly. Back to silence.

"What the..." started Kelly.

""I don't know, but I'm pretty sure we're gonna find out," replied Harry. "And to answer your question Teale, I think we just became someone's lunch."

Kelly didn't hear the dripping until it was almost in front of her. A steady drip, drip, drip was pattering onto the previously shiny and new marble floor. She aimed her disruptor rifle above, the beam of the torch attached illuminating the target. There was no question about it. The liquid was blood. And it was dripping through the light fixture above them, which now glowed the red of danger as opposed to its usual halo of white. Reluctantly, Kelly nodded to one of her security team, and he leaned up, unclipping the fitting. With only half the bolts removed, the sheer weight above buckled the rest of the fitting and the entire ceiling panel came crashing down from above, the security officer being knocked to the ground by the appearance of what used to be a human body.

Kelly wanted to scream, but she forced herself to keep it in. The mangled corpse was pushed aside by the security officer, and Kelly couldn't tear her eyes away from the horror which lay in front of her. There was no face left to speak of. Four deep claw marks were scratched into the skull beneath, and similar marks tore through the chest of the victim. A large pool of blood began to collect around the body, and Kelly noticed one of its legs had been torn away, the tendons and muscles hanging limply from the severed thigh. Very quietly, she addressed her team.

"Grant and Sanderson, you two fan out towards engineering. Grayson and Hunt, you two head for Cargo Bay One. Teale, you and me will head for sickbay. Keep your wits about you. We don't know what these things are, or where they're hiding. And for the love of god... don't let them touch you."

Silent nods around the group, and the six team members split up heading for their various targets. Only two of the team would return to the bridge when the searches were done.

Harry's team had remained on the bridge to establish if any of the internal sensors were working. They weren't. The Darla had locked everything out before the power drain, so even if they did have full energy capacity, they still wouldn't be able to access main computer systems. After trying and failing to send out a distress call, they had left the bridge and headed in the opposite direction to Kelly's team, towards the crew quarters. With an original crew of a thousand, the quarters made up half the ship's mass. Similarly to Kelly's team, Harry split his into three search parties of two. He teamed up with tactical officer Perry, in the hopes he was as good with a handheld weapon as he was with the ship's disruptor cannons.

"You doing alright back there Lieutenant?" Harry whispered under his breath.

"Yes Sir. Just another day at the office right?"

Harry chuckled to himself, a welcome relief given the circumstances. They turned the corner ahead of them and Harry let out a long sigh, lowering his weapon in frustration.

"Well, that's a dead end then."

In front of them was the only remaining damage from the initial Darla attack months earlier. A ten metre gap in the hull spanning the floor ahead prevented them from going any further. The emergency power had kept the forcefield in place, but it meant they had to find another way around.

Suddenly, a dark shadow shot behind Perry. The light breeze made him spin around, aiming his rifle into the darkness.

"What was that?" he said, his voice trembling.

"I didn't see anything Lieutenant. Are you sure?"

Perry turned back to Harry.

"I felt something behind me Sir, like a... a shadow."

Harry's own heart rate was elevated so he knew how Perry was feeling. This was after all, his first deep space mission of any kind. The *Odyssey* had plucked him straight out of the academy. Tested off the charts second only to Commander Kelly Dresden. Harry had chosen him personally. Promoted him within six weeks, and stationed him at tactical.

"This constant darkness has us all on edge, son. But I'm still not picking up any lifeforms on my scanner. It's just your mind playing tricks on you."

Perry chuckled and shook his head.

"Forgive me Admiral Ransome, but I've seen this movie, and the black dude gets it first. If it's all the same to you, I'd appreciate you checking it out with me."

"Lieutenant Jayden Perry, are you asking me to hold your hand?"

The levity was welcomed and it broke a good degree of the tension, as Harry nodded and the two of them returned to the junction they had turned around moments earlier. Harry wanted to keep Perry distracted as long as possible, and himself if he was being honest. He decided to make small talk.

"So Jayden, what did your old man think of you making it onto the *Odyssey*?" he asked.

"He couldn't be prouder, Sir. He wanted to come to your house and shake your hand personally. It was everything I could do to get him to stay home."

Harry chuckled as he swept his torch light across what he thought was a figure in the darkness. It was in fact a discarded fire extinguisher.

"I served with your dad on Mars. He was a good soldier. Always first into the barracks of a morning, and last one out. I was real sorry about what happened to him."

Perry nodded his head as he too aimed his flashlight at a moving shadow up ahead.

"He's doing alright Sir. We had the house adapted, and now he rolls his ass around the place like a Formula E driver."

Harry pictured the very image in his mind. Marcus Perry had always been a speed demon. He was planning to test the next iteration of the star drive once his tour of duty was completed. Unfortunately a rogue disruptor blast at maximum power across his spine put that dream beyond reach.

Whoosh.

Something flew behind Perry, this time much closer than it had been before. He span round to try and catch it, Harry turning with him.

Whoosh.

This time, behind Harry. And this time he felt it. The hairs on the nape of his neck shot towards the sky, and goosebumps covered his whole body.

"I guess it wasn't your imagination, Jayden."

"No Sir, it was not."

From behind Perry, a scratching sound started echoing towards them. It got gradually louder as it came closer to them, and the sound equivalent to nails on a chalkboard almost shattered Ransome and Perry's eardrums, such was the volume. And then it stopped, leaving the two of them staring into the darkness, their breathing the only audible sound.

Whoosh.

"AAAAAAAAAAAARRRRRGGGHHHHHHHH!!!!!"

In the blink of an eye, Jayden Perry was gone, his rifle clattered to the floor, and only a trail of blood as evidence he had ever been there in the first place. His cries only audible for a moment, but enough for Harry to have a rough direction to head in. The speed of the attack had, for a moment, failed to register in Harry's mind. He had never even seen Perry move, never mind the creature which had taken him. But as he stalked around the next corner in the corridor, a thought occurred to him which until now, hadn't.

On a ship of a thousand people, where was everybody else?

THIRTEEN

The sickbay was a mess. Literally and figuratively. Kelly and Teale arrived to find one of the doors hanging off its hinges and the other in a constant state of opening and closing. Sliding between the malfunctioning door, they quickly established they should've stayed outside. Every single bio-bed had been destroyed. Either broken in half or launched across the room. Beneath the wreckage were several severed limbs, varying in size and type, but Kelly counted at least two dozen. Directly above the pile was an enormous hole in the ceiling, three light panels ripped free to create the gap.

"We're being hunted," she said out loud to Teale, who shrugged her injured arm free of her sling. "What are you doing?"

Teale swung her shoulder around a few times to achieve some mobility.

"Figured I'd probably need two hands for whatever shit we're about to get into. Besides, no offence Sir, but if you go to shoot me again, this is my punching arm."

Kelly smiled briefly, before moving toward the pile of human remains. Blood stained the outline of the hole, and Kelly could see in the beam of her rifle torch that the hole went right through to the deck above. It looked as if something had simply torn its way through the metal.

A beep emanated from Kelly's wrist communicator.

"Go ahead."

"Commander, we've just reached engineering. You're gonna wanna see this, Sir."

Deciding there was nothing they could do here, Kelly and Teale made their way back out into the hallway, but a loud clang from behind them in sickbay stopped them in their tracks. Kelly gestured for Teale to wait in the corridor, and she stepped back inside. Another clang, from somewhere inside the chief medical officer's room. Kelly could make out a gargling noise, and she knew somebody was in there. She took one step further, and under her foot, a shattered beaker crunched loudly. She stopped dead.

"Shit."

The glass in the office erupted outwards as a mangled torso was thrown from the room, landing in a heap, the brittle and damaged bones audibly cracking on impact. But it was the beast that followed the body through the now broken window that made Kelly's blood run cold. The creature stood at least eight feet tall, perhaps more, and its torso appeared to be armoured. Whether it was artificial or part of an exoskeleton, she couldn't tell. It's head was similar to a humanoid design, but had an elongated look, sweeping back tightly from the face. It's hands were claws with six inch talons on each of the four fingers, and the feet were the same, but four times the size. The claws on the feet were actually tearing into the floor as the creature turned to look at Kelly.

It's face was a contorted construction. No lips to speak of, but long yellowed razor sharp teeth spanned the gap in two rows, drool cascading from the mouth onto the floor. And the eyes. They were a piercing red, almost glowing like fire. Kelly was so transfixed by the stature of this alien creature, that she had failed to notice its scorpion-like tail whipping through the air. The blade like fins attached to the tail sliced three large gashes into Kelly's arm, and she dropped her rifle falling to the floor in agony. Again, the tail whipped through the air, but she just managed to roll out of the way as it cut clean through the floor where she had been just seconds before. Wasting no time, she scrambled to her feet, and fumbled her way through the darkness clutching her arm, the blood seeping between her fingers as she headed back towards the exit.

"Teale! Run! Get out of here!" she screamed.

She heard a scrambling noise, and the sound of more metal twisting behind her. She dared to look over her shoulder and found the edge of the creature's tail vanishing up into the hole in the ceiling. The savaged torso was also gone. As Kelly fell through the door into the corridor, Teale rushed over to her.

"Oh my god, are you alright? What the fuck was that thing?" she spluttered as she tried to wrap her sling around Kelly's arm as a bandage.

"I don't know, but we have to get the fuck out of here. Screw engineering, we're going back to the bridge."

Almost as if on cue, the first team that had been assigned to engineering, rounded the corner at pace.

"Commander! There's some kind of... nest in engineering! We tried to take a reading, but they started to open up, so we ran. Whatever these things are, they're fast. We passed the cargo bay on the way, and they were... eating Grayson and Hunt!"

What the fuck were these things? Nests? They'd only been in the expanse for a matter of hours... hadn't they? Either way, the bridge was the safest place. But they wouldn't all make it.

The tip of the tail burst through Sanderson's chest like a medieval sword, his back arching in response. Blood began to flow through his mouth like a waterfall as he was lifted gradually from the floor, one of the creatures standing behind him. The tail jerked to the left, and Sanderson's trembling body was launched against the bulkhead, his neck snapping as his head collided with the metal first.

Before anyone could react, the tail sliced through the air again, and the sound of tearing flesh filled their senses as Grant was sliced in two from the top of the skull through to the ground. Kelly watched in horror as the two halves of the security officer fell apart in opposite directions. Something came over Teale, and she opened fire on the creature, screaming as she did so. The hallway lit up with the constant stream of disruptor fire, and the creature for a moment seemed to weather the assault. It then seemed to think better of it, and turned and leapt upwards, before spearing its tail downwards again, to collect first the skewered body of Sanderson, and then swiftly returned for the two pieces of officer Grant.

Kelly and Teale didn't look back. They ran, and ran until they reached the bridge, more screams echoing down the corridors all over the ship.

FOURTEEN

THE GATHERING on the bridge was a sombre one. Of course there was panic running through the very fibres of everyone in the room, but the overwhelming loss they had suffered was simply unfathomable. The bridge was the only place on the ship which could be entirely isolated from all other areas. It was also, should the need arise, the first module design of any starship, or space faring craft. Upon command authorisation from three senior officers, the bridge module could be separated from the rest of the ship. In effect, it was a very powerful Captain's Yacht. And it was this very notion which Harry Ransome was now dismissing.

"But Admiral, you've seen these things. Whatever they are, they've adapted to our weapons, we can't track them, and in a matter of hours, they've slaughtered a crew of nearly a thousand!"

Kelly Dresden's voice reached pitches even she didn't know she could reach. Her own experiences had told her to get the fuck out of dodge, and yet for some reason, their commanding officer was refusing to leave.

"I know Commander."

Infuriated, Kelly threw the chain of command to the wind and launched a foul mouthed tirade at Harry, laced with expletives, and mistakes she felt he had made in pursuing the Darla craft that attacked them. Her rant garnered some groans of support, several wounded officers nodding their heads. Harry listened to every word she said, not breaking eye contact for a single moment.

"Are you done, Commander?" he asked calmly.

Kelly had nothing left. Her arm was throbbing, despite the wound being healed thanks to an emergency bridge medi-pack. But her argument had been delivered, and now she had exhausted what little remaining energy she had. Slumping into her own seat at the Operations console, she rested her head in her hands.

"Good. Now I understand that many of you wish to leave the *Odyssey* and fire us out of here on emergency thrusters. But that is not an option. There are thirty-six of you in here, right now. My scanner reports at least twenty more human bio-signs scattered throughout the ship. Put yourself in your fellow crew members shoes. Would you want to be left behind?"

Muffled noises suggesting the officers present would rather not answer, travelled around the bridge. But Harry wasn't done.

"Exactly. Now there is another part of the ship's design that is privy only to me, the designer, and the Chief of Security. It is only to be used in an emergency situation, and when I say emergency, I mean *dire* emergency."

Harry looked up towards the ceiling, and scanned the surface for something. Everyone followed his gaze, but saw nothing in the dim red glow of the emergency lights. Moments later, Harry found what he was looking for. He withdrew his disruptor rifle from its resting place against the side of his chair, aimed it at the section he had been focussing on, and fired a single shot. Sparks flew down from above as everyone cowered, but the result of the shot surprised them even more.

The dim red lights were deactivated, and were replaced with a deep ocean blue, making the entire room feel as if everyone were under water. The lights were static, which came as a relief to those who were beginning to get migraines from the pulsing effect they'd spent the last several hours staring at. Harry strode back to his chair.

"Computer, emergency preservation order one. Confirm availability, authorisation Ransome, Tango-Alpha-Seven-Four."

A brief silence.

"Authorisation confirmed. Emergency Preservation Order One is available. Request deployment or protocol details."

The fact that there was available power surprised most, but the fact that there was an entirely secret protocol hidden within the ship was causing everyone to wonder what else the Utopia founders were hiding.

"Display protocol details, main viewscreen, include schematics."

"Acknowledged."

The viewscreen switched from the external view of nothing, to a split screen. One displayed what looked like an instruction manual, but details specific points of the preservation order. Harry gestured towards the screen, and everyone shuffled forward to read it.

"Are those schematics... for cryogenic suspension pods?" asked Teale.

"More or less, Commander," replied Harry, patiently waiting for everyone to finish dissecting what they were seeing. "The *Odyssey* was designed for long service, and as such, it was anticipated that we may need a way to suspend ourselves in order to travel further. There are no families on these ships, and so we are all there would be. Not much use finding an inhabitable planet if by the time you arrive you're ninety years old."

Kelly turned on him.

"Why wasn't I briefed? I outrank the Security Chief. You didn't trust me with this?"

Harry shook his head.

"I opposed the system, Kelly. I remember the failed attempts at cryo-stasis during the wars. We lost some good people when it all went to shit. So I said no. The President overruled me. I only discovered the system had been installed anyway by accident. Even Drusilla isn't aware I know. Before all of this kicked off, I had planned a meeting with you to discuss how best we could remove it. But now, seems like our only hope."

Kelly softened at his words of encouragement. She had not been intentionally left out of the loop. Not with this information, anyway.

"This seems far more complex than those old tubes though Harry. How does it work exactly?"

Harry stood up and used his rifle as a pointer, explaining the finer points of the system. It also explained how the Security Chief was briefed but nobody else.

"Essentially," Harry concluded, "each pod is a self contained shuttlecraft. Independent life support, food supplies, even a disruptor cannon albeit on a far smaller scale. Think of it as a one man escape pod, but it puts you to sleep too. In the event the ship's integrity is compromised, while the crew was under, it would eject each pod into space, and activate the homing protocol. It was designed to take its occupant back to Earth. Obviously on thrusters that would take lifetimes, but in cryo-stasis that doesn't matter. The introduction of weapons and shields was known only by the chosen Security Chief of each vessel."

Finally able to take in all this information, it was Commander Teale who seemed to take charge of the conversation.

"So I'm presuming you intend to use this system in some capacity Admiral? Or are we meant to all stand around here with metaphorical dicks in our hands, waiting for these ugly bastards to fuck off?"

A mixture of surprised and impressed faces caused Harry to

smirk. This one was a great asset to the team, and he still regretted the fact he was unable to convince her to join security.

"You're damn right Teale. I intend to put you all inside the cryopods get you safely under, and then go and find the rest of my crew."

Immediate protests came flying his way, first from Teale, then from several junior officers, and the from Kelly Dresden.

"No."

"No?"

"You deaf? I said no. Fuck rank and fuck protocol. Right now Harry, you have a hugely dwindled crew, and aliens who can move through this ship undetected and unaffected by our defences. And you want to lock away those who are left and go hunting on your own? I don't think so."

Harry was furious at the amount of open defiance from his crew, but he simply knew they were right. The furious side of him was the rule obeying, academy graduate. But the realistic side of him was the man of experience. He knew Dresden was right. The question was, how many could he risk. He had already seen several officers, good officers, eviscerated, sliced up and full on eaten. He took a moment, followed by a deep breath, and decided he would create a team of four.

"You're right. As usual."

Kelly smirked, then winced as she moved her injured arm too quickly and felt the regenerated skin pull tight.

"Computer, deploy Preservation Order One."

"*Deployment in progress.*"

As everyone watched, the ceiling of the bridge began to open up. The seams had been extremely well hidden, but once the doors had revealed their contents, dozens of pods began to slide down from above.

"Commanders Dresden and Teale, you're with me."

He glanced around the room, but there were several faces he still didn't know.

"Our Security Chief is dead. Who was second in command of that division?"

A small cough emanated from the back of the crowd, and the officers parted to let them through.

"That would be me Admiral."

A tall man, no more than late twenties stepped forward. His uniform had been torn in several places, revealing what appeared to be tribal markings on his arms. The man himself had a close shaved beard or darkest black, and long hair which was tied up in a tight ponytail as per regulation. There was steel in his eyes, and Harry wondered how he had not met this young man earlier. He certainly would have remembered.

"What's your name, son?" asked Harry.

The man stood feet shoulder width apart, and back straight.

"Knight, Sir. Lieutenant Joshua Knight."

FIFTEEN

THE SIGHT WAS one of the most evil and depraved nightmares. The sheer volume of blood, and severed body parts scattered all around him, made him feel as if he couldn't possibly be awake. Nothing in the universe could be this grotesque and malevolent. And yet here he was. Standing on his own bridge, on his own ship. The pain Darven felt in his temples, also made him very aware he was in fact still in reality, albeit one of death.

"Why me?" he pleaded, straining his voice, tears flowing down his face, catching in the ridges on his nose.

"You are different..."

The voice sounded almost simulated, but there was definite menace in each word, spoken as if through a clenched jaw.

"I don't understand!" Darven pleaded again. "I've done nothing to warrant survival! Please leave my mind and just let me die like the rest!"

The creatures had forced Darven to deliver his entire fleet into the Expanse, his own consciousness locked in a cage at the back of his mind as they pulled the strings. He was now the only living Darla in the entire system.

"You knew... her..."

The last word sent shivers running through every part of Darven's body. He knew exactly who the creature meant. Of that there was no doubt.

"I haven't seen her in decades! The last time I saw her, she almost killed me. I was lucky to escape!"

A demonic laughter came from the darkness, the source only ascertained by the dim glow of the red eyes in the distance.

"You know her, you know she sends people here... and you know why..."

Yes, Darven did know that Drusilla was sending humans here. She was using her telepathic abilities to force them to come here. But the alien was wrong. He did not know why. He assumed she was unaware of the presence of these beings, which is why he sent Ransome and his crew here as punishment.

"I do not know why she sends people here, I swear it!"

More maniacal laughter.

"You do... think hard... or let us show you..."

An ear shattering scream erupted from Darven's throat with such force, it tore his vocal chords, blood pooling in his throat. Once again his mind was being invaded, but the images he was being shown by the creatures were worse than nightmares. They were scenes that could only come from the darkest pits of hell. After minutes of head pounding agony, the creatures relinquished their hold on Darven, and he collapsed to the floor, immediately coated in the blood of his eviscerated colleagues. Unable to speak, he thought his words, aware the creatures could hear him.

Why? Why would she do that? To what end?

"Because she is not who she claims to be... she is something far more evil..."

For a creature of this dominance, this bloodthirsty to claim that Drusilla was something worse, chilled Darven's already cold blood. The images he had seen had made him want to vomit uncontrollably. Never before had he seen so much blood, pain, suffering, torture and displays of someone playing god. He forced himself to push the horror to one side, and formed his next thought.

What is it you want me to do?

"Find her and bring her here... and the rest of the humans..."

Humans? Why do you need the humans?

"We must feast..."

With those final words, power was restored to Darven's ship, and when the lights returned, both the creatures and body parts of his crew were gone, leaving only a large amount of blood, an empty ship, and it's shell shocked Captain.

SIXTEEN

There was a stark contrast between the seeming safety of the blue ocean lights on the bridge and the pulsing glow of the blood red emergency lights throughout the rest of the ship. Never before had Harry Ransome felt less safe than he did now. He was prey on his own ship. Although his mind had been made up before they left the bridge, and the thirty-two crew members had been safely hidden in their cryo-pods, his nerves were now starting to show. Sweat pooled on his forehead, and he could feel it trickling down his back. There had also been a distinct rise in the ship's temperature over the last few hours. So much so, that Harry, Kelly, Teale and Knight had all shed their uniform jackets, choosing to patrol in their black under vests instead. Knight suggested the colour change would give them a more tactical advantage. Harder to see black in the dark. He knew it was nonsense, given these creatures abilities, but it made everyone feel better. Harry made a note to get to know this young man, if they survived.

"Lifesigns up ahead," Kelly whispered. "Four humans, looks like the mess hall."

Harry nodded to Knight and Teale, and they both took up flanking positions at the junction of the corridor. So far they had heard no movement, and no sign of the aliens. Standing directly in front of the door to the mess, Harry handed his rifle to Kelly, and began to prise the doors open with his hands. He knew there were emergency release devices located in the bulkheads nearby to make this job easier, but they daren't split up from each other. Besides, Harry was in good shape, and soon, the doors began to part. When the gap was wide enough, Harry slipped inside, and Kelly passed his rifle through the gap to him. She gestured for Knight and Teale to head inside, and covered them while they did so. Once inside, all four aimed their rifles ahead, the lights on the weapons illuminating similar devastation to Sickbay.

Tables were smashed into pieces, glass fragments everywhere, and countless food items littering every surface. Again, there was a large hole visible in the roof at the mid-way point in the room, the twisted metal at its edges giving Kelly flashbacks to her earlier attack.

Suddenly, there was a loud clatter to their right, and a tin of soup rolled into the beam of Knight's torch. The can was coated in blood. He gestured to the others, and gradually, keeping a constant sweep around them, they moved forward towards the source of the sound. Another noise, this time the sound of a cupboard hinge whining. It reminded Harry of the ancient horror movies he had watched as a teenager where the creaking of a door would often signal a character's impending doom. He could not help but draw comparisons to their current situation. However, the rifle torches found a half open supply cupboard, no doubt the origin of the mysterious tin of soup.

"Open it," Harry gestured to Knight, who nodded in reply.

With a swift lunge, Knight leapt forward and ripped the cupboard door open, three officers in various states of health tumbling onto the floor in a heap.

"No! Get away from us! Get away!" one of them screamed.

"It's okay! We're hear to help!" Kelly whispered as loudly as she dared.

It took a few seconds for the others to realise just who they were looking at, before one of them attempted to salute the Admiral. He shook his head and lowered the saluting hand with his own.

"No need for that crewman. We need to get you out of here. Our scanner showed a fourth person. Are they not with you?"

The cupboard dwellers shook their head in unison.

"It's just been us three for the last two hours. It's the only place we could find to get out of sight. They... they're in the walls."

Harry nodded, fairly confident already that the creatures were using the maintenance tunnels to get around the *Odyssey*. But most of them were too small, hence the holes in the ceilings between decks.

"Sir," interrupted Teale, "I'm still reading a fourth lifesign."

The team swept their beams before them, but it didn't take long to locate the fourth person. It was Harry's torch that landed on the face of the female officer in question. Her abdomen had been all but shredded, blood pooling around her. Both legs were gone, as were her arms, and her left eye was nothing more than a congealed mess of flesh and fluid. The mouth was taking in quick, short breaths, as if she was hyperventilating. But it was Knight's torch which illuminated the true horror. Pressed against the throat of the female officer, was an enormous black foot, the claws at the end embedded in the woman's shoulder. As all four lights moved up to show the alien in all it's glory, it bared its teeth, and lifted its foot. As it did so, a huge stream of blood flowed upwards like a fountain from the throat of the woman. Within seconds, she was dead.

They had been baited.

"Mother fucker," spat Knight. "It kept her alive to lure us here."

Almost in response it seemed, the creature appeared to smile. They all heard the sinister voice in their heads.

"Clever boy."

Kelly ushered the found crewmen out through the doors of the mess hall, but as each one exited, a dark shadow burst past the door, snatching them away, blood spraying up the walls as each one was lifted into oblivion. They were now trapped. And the creatures knew it. Again, Harry felt the voice intruding his thoughts.

"Hello... Harry..."

Hearing the creature say his name terrified Harry to his very core. It began to move slowly towards him, taking one huge footstep at a time, the complete opposite to what he knew of these creatures. The others had not been privy to the mental voice note Harry had received, and Kelly tugged on his arm.

"What is it Harry?"

Harry tensed up and took a step back.

"It knows my name."

"We wondered when you would join us..."

Pain burst through Harry's temple, and he dropped his rifle. He heard manic laughter in his head and he tried to shake it away but he couldn't. The creatures outside the mess hell were now slashing through the metal, trying to create a big enough gap to fit through. The one already in the room was now mere steps from Harry and the others, and Kelly was on the ground desperately trying to shake Harry back into focus. This was it, thought Teale. This is where they died.

Except... they didn't.

There was a huge jolt as something rocked the ship, violently. Everyone was knocked off their feet and sent careening into the wall, the creatures also losing their footing. An odd look of confusion was etched onto their black, gleaming faces. Their heads seemed to gesture to each other as if they were communicating in the same way they had done to Harry. Another jolt, and everything seemed to tilt to the left, debris on the floor rolling into the team, the broken glass and discarded tins smashing into them, slicing and bruising their bodies.

With no warning, the creature which had spoken to Harry let out a shrill scream, which was joined by the others, and as if fired from a cannon, they all launched themselves upwards through the ceiling and out of sight. The scrabbling of their claws on the decks above grew ever more distant as they fled.

"What the fuck is going on?" shouted Knight.

"I've got no idea, but one thing I do know," Kelly said, "is that somehow, we're moving!"

A bleep came from Harry's communicator, now relocated to his belt from his sleeve. His head was still swimming with confusion and residual pain, but he managed to activate the device.

"Who is this?" he managed, failing to get up off the floor and landing on a shard of broken glass, wincing with the pain.

"Admiral Ransome, this is Darven. Hold tight, I'm getting you out of here!"

The communication cut off, but the stunned look in the room from everyone screamed one thing. Nobody knew what the fuck was going on.

SEVENTEEN

THE RED AND blue pattern wasn't quite the same, but Harry appreciated the work the tailor had done on the garment. It was almost a perfect match. Although a large part of him wondered if he preferred not to don his uniform again. After all, it was a symbol of betrayal and death. But, given the efforts the kind people of Santana Prime had gone to in order to help him and his remaining crew, he decided he would wear it. At least once.

It had been a long journey to this point. After their rescue from the Expanse by Darven, Harry and the others had learned there were actually almost two hundred survivors on board the *Odyssey*. Still, that meant eight hundred lives had been lost. And for what? They still didn't know. Darven had refused to explain to them what he had seen. He was clearly incredibly disturbed after his own experiences in the Expanse. He did explain how he had managed to suppress the invasion of his mind long enough to lock on an energy tether and pull them clear. Something the creatures were not impressed with, he could tell. They had fled the *Odyssey* as it approached the golden nebula and attempted to infiltrate Darven's mind once more, but his increasing distance helped keep his safeguards in place. The Darla Captain had sent them on their way, before fleeing himself, but had failed to give them the access codes to their lockout. This meant thruster travel. For three months.

Finding themselves here, was a miracle. Not only that, but to find an intact colony willing to trade was invaluable. The people of Santana Prime had made it clear they could not stay, as they had limited resources themselves, but it was part of their custom to never turn away those in need of help. The ship was all but repaired, the bodies of fallen crew relocated to the cargo bays in proper caskets, ready for burial among the stars, and food supplies had been topped up. With the lockouts now broken, Harry was free to resume whatever journey he saw fit. And yet he was troubled.

He couldn't shake the feeling of discomfort at the alien creature knowing his name. There had been a tinge of the artificial to the sound of the voice, but also a touch of familiarity. In order to move forward, he tried to put it down to something he must have picked up from Drusilla while their minds were joined previously. After all, it was her who he assumed had planned to send them to the Expanse eventually, as Darven had alluded to when they first met.

"Ship is ready to go Admiral."

Commander, now Captain Kelly Dresden, stood alongside Harry, in a straight stance, hands clasped behind her back, and her blonde hair in a perfect bun, not a hair out of place.

"Well then, Captain, let's get back to it."

Kelly nodded, still proud of Harry's promotion of her, despite the haunting of their experiences. The *Odyssey* was hers now, Harry deciding to take a backseat advisory role. He needed time to think. About what came next. Where he should go. What future there was for them out here. And where and when Drusilla might turn up again.

The Santana Prime engineers had done wonders. The *Odyssey* sat on a landing gantry the size of New York City with three other ships of differing design. She looked brand new. No exterior damage visible, new weaponry, new shielding, and even a special gift from the Prime Minister of the outpost – a cloaking device.

Inside was the same. The bridge was even more advanced than it had been originally. There were now two chairs in the centre of the room. The Captain's chair which would now be occupied by Kelly, and the First Officer's chair, which would be occupied by Harry, despite another promotion for Commander Teale. She had generously donated her new chair to the Admiral until the completion of their journey, although nobody was sure of how long that would be.

The crew was down to just one-hundred-sixty-five upon departure, dozens succumbing to their wounds after landing. Positions were promoted, and shuffled around, and Teale was trained in security to serve alongside Joshua Knight, who was the new Chief. Harry had a good feeling about those two. In the near calendar year they had been here, Knight and Teale had gotten very close. He had considered advising against inner ship relations, but given what they had been through, he decided everyone deserved a little happiness however long it lasted.

As they left orbit, leaving the moon outpost of Santana Prime behind them, they did not realise that their happiness would stretch to almost a full decade. Travelling among the stars, meeting new species, and even an encounter with one of the other starships, the *Valiant*. But like everything else, all good things must come to an end. And almost ten years to the day of their departure from Earth, the end came swift, brutal, and unforgiving.

EIGHTEEN

THERE WAS a distinct air of betrayal surrounding both Harry and Drusilla as they sat in the same quarters that years ago they had made love in. Looking back on those times, Harry now wondered if he had willingly succumbed to those tender moments, or if it was more of Drusilla's manipulative influences on his mind. Several times over the past decade, he had found himself trying to remember any lead up to those encounters, and often found himself drawing a blank. Of one thing, however, he was certain. He had no feelings of any kind for her now. Except contempt.

After eight years of blissful exploration with his remaining crew, Harry had received a tip-off from an acquaintance he had made on the trading station Azanti Prime. Someone was looking for him, and she had taken out three staff members to try and elicit the location of the *Odyssey*. Harry had known immediately that it was Drusilla. He ordered a change in course and for the last eighteen months, they had been fleeing. That's when it started.

During a deep sleep in the middle of the night, Harry would hear whispers in his ear. Promises that she would see him again soon. He had no idea how powerful Drusilla's powers were, but he surmised they were extremely potent to reach him from such distance. One of the crew, an Ensign Colbeck, had retrained to become their new Chief Medical Officer, and Harry had sought him out to try and stop these messages from coming through. But in the end, it made no difference. Just a matter of hours ago, he sensed she was close. He ordered their pilot to push the engines to the max, but it wasn't enough to outrun Drusilla's talons. In a moment of blackout, she had commandeered Harry's mind, and forced him to knock out the pilot, alter course, and stun three of his crew before releasing him. By that time, they were already on board.

"What's the matter Harry? You used to be happy to see me."

Her voice no longer held the soft and melancholic tones of the woman he once knew.

"Something tells me Dru, I was never willingly happy to see you. And certainly not now."

Drusilla puckered her face in a mock display of hurt.

"Well that's not very nice is it? At least your wife was happy to see me when I paid her a visit."

The words hung in the air, Harry unsure how to process them. He had thought about Annette and Findlay quite often recently, often wondering if he was betraying them by continuing in his new life.

"What did you do?" he questioned, words low and harsh coming slowly from his lips.

Drusilla slid a white blade from a sheath on her hip, and twirled it in the air, catching it by the tip.

"Just tying up a few... loose ends."

The smile that spread across her face was almost demonic, and Harry lunged at her, but his eyes glazed over, and he stopped mid stride, slowly turning back to his seat and lowering himself into it calmly. When Drusilla released his mind, the fury returned, but he stayed seated.

"And my son?" he spat through clenched teeth.

"Yes, terrible shame. So full of honour, that one. I'm sure he would've made an excellent commanding officer one day. Never mind."

Pain and torment tore through Harry, knowing that the woman he had betrayed them for, that he had turned his back on them for, had killed them both in cold blood. He bit back his response, but a tear did fall down his cheek. There would be time for grieving later. His crew was at stake now.

"What do you want from us?" he said, thinking each word as he focussed on it, making sure he didn't say anything that would cause another invasion of his mind.

"I already told you Harry. You don't listen well do you?"

"You said you wanted our humanity. You didn't elaborate."

Drusilla stood up and strolled around the room, digging under her nails with the blade as if it were a tool for manicuring.

"You know, for a man fucking his Captain, you're awfully tense."

That knocked the wind out of Harry's sails. Clearly he had not been protecting his thoughts enough. The very second he showed inner concern for Kelly Dresden, she had latched onto it.

"That's none of your concern."

Drusilla smiled once again.

"Oh, but it is Harry! It's a perfect example of humanity. The ability to adapt to new surroundings, environments and circumstances. To be inventive when the need arises, to explore the human condition! That... that is what I've been looking for all these years!"

The concern for Kelly grew. Harry had only been officially in a relationship with his former first officer for the last twelve months, and only then after much soul searching and the realisation that they were never heading home. He now feared she was about to become a pawn in Drusilla's games.

"Hooray, we're clever. So are countless other species. Far more so than us. I've met them. So why *us*?"

Drusilla rounded on him and brought the knife to within millimetres of his throat, causing him to lean back in his chair.

"Because you don't break."

She leaned back from Harry, the blade having nicked his neck slightly, but enough that a single thin line of blood formed on his throat. Drusilla continued.

"Whatever is thrown at your species, you face it head on. Even through denial, and depression, waves and waves of anxiety, the species continues. You're resilient, Harry. Other species simply don't come up to the same levels. And this has to go *perfectly*."

Harry allowed his rage to bubble to the surface along with a great deal of impatience.

"For fuck's sake, just tell me what you want us for!" he yelled.

Drusilla was not a fan of being on the receiving end of any retaliation, either physical or verbal. Harry didn't even have time to blink, before she was upon him. Gripping him with one hand around his throat, and the other grabbing the waist of his trousers, she hauled him into the air, and slammed his back down through the desk they were sat near. The metal didn't simply bend, it fractured apart as Harry's spine tore through it. She hovered over his weary body, his face contorted in pain, and spat her next words callously.

"I'm going to make every single one of your fucking lackeys out there into something far more powerful! Something that not even they could comprehend! The rest of your precious fleet is already undergoing the process, and by the time I'm done, the only humanity left in this universe will be bottled and in my hand!"

She retrieved the small blade, twirled it in her hand three-sixty, and plunged it down into Harry's left shoulder, the tip of the blade scraping the bone as it pierced his muscle. The scream brought her extreme pleasure, and she leaned in once more.

"If you don't send that message to Earth, I'm going to slice the throat of every single person on this ship. And I'm going to start with your little mistress. But the best part? I'm going to make you do it!"

Harry spat at her as she stood and moved away from him. His strength was being driven by rage, and he had every possible desire for vengeance running through his veins. Against better judgement, he gripped the handle of the knife and tore it from his shoulder, blood pulsing out from the wound as he did so. His screams could be heard all around the ship. He threw the blade to one side and dragged himself up against the now destroyed metal desk, pain sparking at the base of his spine as he stumbled back towards his chair. Taking several deep and slow, methodical breaths, he turned his glare back to Drusilla.

"Why? Why do you need me to send this message so badly? You clearly don't need to use us, you have more than enough ability to subdue us. God knows you've done it enough already."

He saw a flash of an image in his mind of his wife and son screaming for mercy as Drusilla stood over their bloodied bodies cackling, her electric blue hair waving in the breeze. He blinked it away and a tear went with it.

"One simple reason, my dear. *Despair*. For the genius I have planned for humans, necessary conditions need to be put in place. For the rest of *Utopia*, they have each been placed into individual circumstances to create unique... conditions to study. For you and your crew, it will be resilience. For the rest of humanity back on Earth, it will be despair."

Harry tried to follow what she was saying, but as far as he was concerned the woman was talking in riddles. Each time he tried to comprehend what she was talking about, he simply couldn't grasp a solid concept. However, his mission was clear. His crew were in immediate danger. And the people of Earth were next. He had set out a decade ago to save humanity. That mission had not changed, despite him and his crew losing their way. He could not trick his way out of this, and he needed to buy time. There was only one option he could take at this moment. He took a deep breath, and spat the words from between gritted teeth.

"I'll send your fucking message."

NINETEEN

THE LEVEL of deception which Drusilla had designed was far more intense than Harry could have ever imagined. She ordered him to record not one, but two messages to Earth. One now, and one to remain on an automated state of readiness in the *Odyssey*'s computer banks. Both were complete fabrications blaming the Darla for luring them to their deaths. While certain information was factual, such as the number of remaining crew, and their experiences within the Expanse, Drusilla was trying to create something that was foolproof. Blaming the Darla would take suspicion away from her, whilst providing a legitimate enemy with a grudge to bear that was entirely believable. It would also instil fear into those who saw the messages, that hope of rescue was gone, creating the conditions she desired for whatever lay ahead.

But it went even further than that. She had falsified crew logs typed out and randomly redacted sections, creating the illusion of some kind of paranoid conspiracy on board the ship, again leading to the belief that the Darla were to blame. It soon became very clear that Drusilla had not been planning this for years, she'd been planning it for *decades.*

It took six days for everything to fall into place, and prepare the *Odyssey* for its next journey. In that time, the remaining crew had been individually isolated in crew quarters, while Harry was chained to his chair on the bridge under constant watch. As he glanced over to where Lieutenant Joshua Knight's body had fallen, he felt a pang of sadness in his core. They had become a family over the last nine years. Now they had lost one of their own. And it hurt like hell. He could only imagine how hard Teale was finding it having watched her partner executed just to prove a point. Harry wasn't even sure what they had done with his body. With a stealthy shuffle, Drusilla was beside him, inches from his face.

"It's time, Harry. Our journey is complete, and there is somebody you and your friends need to meet."

Before Harry could say anything, his chains were unlocked, and he was grabbed by two men who hauled him upright and dragged him off the bridge. He struggled against his captors as they carried him through the ship, but they were too strong, and he too weak.

"Where are you taking me?" he yelled at the men. "Where are we going?"

One of the men delivered a swift fist to his stomach, and Harry doubled over.

"Shut the fuck up!"

When Harry looked up, he saw the large doors to the cargo bay opening, and inside, all of his remaining crew were huddled together. The two men launched Harry into the room, and he landed on his shoulder, exacerbating the knife wound which although healed with a med kit, still ached substantially. The two men then turned, and left, the doors closing behind them and a forcefield appearing over the doors to prevent escape.

Teale was the first to rush over and check on the Admiral.

"Sir, are you alright?" she asked, gently trying to prop him up into a sitting position.

He motioned to her that he could manage, and tapped his hand against her arm. A look of unspoken apology was passed between the two, but again, the grieving could happen later. He knew Teale had more reason to live than some of the others, and he would make sure of it.

"Where is Captain Dresden?" he asked, coughing sharply as he spoke the words.

Teale did not answer immediately. She looked down at the floor, before bringing her gaze off to the left. Harry followed the motion of her head, and saw near the wall opposite, there was what looked like a medical stretcher, and Ensign Colbeck was stood over it. Teale found her words.

"Drusilla didn't like her attitude... so they made an example of her."

Panic and rage swirled in Harry's gut like a maddening tempest of emotions, and he fought through the pain in his own body and launched himself towards the doctor. When he got there, his entire body froze.

Captain Kelly Dresden had been *destroyed*.

Her hair was mangled, knotted and entirely consumed with her own blood, and in several places appeared to have been torn from her scalp. Her right eye was gone, her left swollen shut. Her nose had clearly been broken and sat at a jarring angle on her face, and both cheeks were swollen, blackened and sporting several gashes that Harry suspected had come from Drusilla's blade.

A blanket was covering her body from the neck down, but by some miracle, Harry saw she was breathing. He turned to Ensign Colbeck, urging him to tell him the full diagnosis of the woman he had come to love. Reluctantly, the doctor filled him in.

"Apart from the damage to her face that you can see, she has a punctured lung, six broken ribs, internal bruising, an irregular heartbeat, seven broken fingers, and one broken wrist, and a shattered left ankle. I'm excellent at what I do, Harry, but without my equipment, all I can do is keep her breathing and out of pain."

Harry touched Colbeck's shoulder, his other hand over his mouth, unable to tear his eyes away from Kelly's traumatised figure. But there was more.

"Harry, they took her tongue."

He knew that it was likely going to cost him his own health, and he knew that a feeling so strong and powerful would be felt by Drusilla on the bridge, but he no longer had control over anything. He screamed in anger and fury, and ran his fist directly through a nearby glass container, sending broken shards everywhere, slicing his hand open. But Harry continued, he tore storage units from the wall, and launched them across the bay. He smashed a control panel on the nearby anti-grav station and tore the wires out, sparks shooting into the air. The crew watched on, every set of eyes filled with sympathy and empathy for their commanding officer. Drusilla had quite literally taken everything from him. All he had left was his crew, and his ship.

Collapsing to the ground in a heap, sobbing into his hands as the blood dripped from them onto the cargo bay floor, Harry was a broken man. Drusilla had said that humans don't break. She was wrong. And here was the proof. But just as quickly as Harry had lost control, he gained a moment of distinct clarity. His eyes scanned the doorway. Sure enough, the communications panel had not been covered by the forcefield. He staggered over to it, ripped off the top panel, and began unplugging wires and computer chips, reinserting them in different locations, until the unmistakable sound of a system powering up could be heard. A smile of determination spread over Harry's face.

"Computer?" he yelled into the vast open space.

"Awaiting commands."

"Open a channel to the bridge."

Drusilla watched eagerly on the viewscreen as the *Odyssey* cleared the perimeter of the Saraswathi Nebula, the golden strands vanishing from view, leaving nothing but darkness before them.

"Stine, are the dampeners in place?" she asked her trigger happy deputy.

"Up and running. The effects of the expanse should be nullified until we reach our destination."

Drusilla smiled. She had not personally ventured into the expanse, but the stories of what lay inside of it gave her cause to ensure they would not fall victim to the same fates as previous travellers. She was now so close to her final destination. Her revenge was in reach. All she had to do, was get there. As she wiped dried blood from her small, white blade, she could not help but think back to when she first met Harry Ransome. Despite everything, and her definite influencing of his mind, she had enjoyed spending time with him. He was a warrior. Of course he had been trained to become one, whereas she had needed to fight and attack in order to become the power she was now. But there was a small part of her that had genuine feelings for him. After all, was that not the reason she had murdered his family? So that he would be hers, and hers alone? That same reasoning had caused her to personally mutilate Captain Kelly Dresden. Harry belonged to *her* and nobody else. Why take such action if there was not more beneath the surface, beneath the vengeance, beneath the blackened heart?

Unfortunately for Drusilla, her thoughts were interrupted by an unauthorised communication from the very man she was conflicted over.

"Drusilla, you fucking bitch. I know you can hear me, and I know you can feel this, so listen to me very carefully."

Harry's voice was almost a growl, and Drusilla could indeed feel the rage and the pain in her very soul, such was its potency. Ordinarily such a strong bond would give her unbridled ecstasy. But not this time. This time, she felt *afraid*.

"You have taken my family. You have taken my home, and you have taken my people. You have butchered the woman I love, and murdered members of my crew. But you know what? You were right. When push comes to shove, humans don't break. And Drusilla? I'm coming for you. I'm going to slice my way through these scumbags you call a crew. I'm going to free my people, and I'm going to wrap my hands around your throat and squeeze the life out of your body until you're on the very cusp of death! And as I watch you die, I'm going to take your knife, and the very last thing you will see is me cutting your heart from your body and holding it in front of you as its blood drips onto the floor! It ends HERE!"

The channel went dead, and the bridge was filled with silence. Drusilla's jaw was actually trembling. She was not fearful of threats and vendettas. She was terrified because she *felt* every word that came from Harry Ransome's lips. And what she felt was the truth. Harry was coming for her.

"Stine, get down to the cargo bay. Kill them all!"

"But Drusilla, you said we needed them-"

"I SAID KILL THEM ALL!"

Stine ran for the doors at the back of the bridge, but before he could get there, the ship jolted violently, as if hit by weapons fire.

"What was that?" asked one of the other men.

"No idea, some kind of energy surge within the ship," answered another.

Then there was a loud clunking noise, the floor of the bridge vibrating underneath them. Every light went out, and every console lost power.

"Wh- what- what is happening?" Drusilla whispered under her breath.

Nobody answered.

"Stine? Report!"

Again, silence.

Drusilla's eyes bulged, and even in the darkness, she could make out the outlines of the consoles in front of her. But there were no people in the seats. Suddenly, there was a rush of air behind her. She spun on the spot, her knife clutched tightly in her right hand.

"Who's there?" she demanded.

A low, guttural growl emerged from somewhere in the darkness, and Drusilla thought she saw a glimpse of red eyes off to her left. She darted forward, but her feet found fresh air, missing the steps down from the command chair in the dark, and she fell onto her front, hard, the blade skittering away from her. Groaning, she rolled onto her back, and hovering directly above her, was the body of every single one of her men, each being held up by something protruding from their chest. The only source of illumination was a rifle torch belonging to Stine, which was jerking violently back and forth as his body spasmed. Rivers of blood flowed down from above, coating Drusilla like water. It filled her eyes, her nose, her mouth, and as she tried to scramble away, it only made her fall back down, this time cracking the side of her head on one of the metal steps. She saw stars and everything swirled around her.

The overwhelming sound of an alarm claxon shattered the silence, and Drusilla threw her hands up to her ears to try and shield her mind from the noise. The siren was then joined by the computer voice.

"Warning, emergency vessel decompression in thirty seconds."

This seemed to elicit a swift response from the alien creatures, who shot back into the hole they had managed to create in the ceiling, dragging along with them the bodies of Drusilla's crew.

"Warning, emergency vessel decompression in twenty seconds."

Drusilla had no idea where she was, her vision still blurred by blood and her head injury. Her hand hit a glowing control panel, and a series of pods came down from the ceiling. The decompression cycle had released the emergency preservation order, and cryo-pods were now descending.

"Warning, emergency vessel decompression in ten seconds."

Drusilla had no idea what was happening, her body seemingly on autopilot. She climbed into one of the pods, completely unaware of her surroundings, the pod sealing itself automatically once she was secured. Inside, a separate automated voice addressed her directly.

"Occupant, do you wish to initiate emergency extraction procedure?"

The side of Drusilla's head was now swollen significantly, and she had lost much blood from the head wound. She could not tell if she was imagining things, hallucinating, or already dead. Somehow, she managed to utter the word, "Yes."

With a violent burst of speed, the pod was ripped from the bridge, and emergency hatch closing behind it, and launched into the empty space beyond the ship. The engines kicked in, and the pod soared at incredible speed back towards the Saraswathi Nebula. As the *Odyssey* became nothing but a tiny speck on the viewscreen of the pod, Drusilla lost consciousness and everything went black.

TWENTY

Three days elapsed before the crew had dared leave the cargo bay. Harry's reconfiguring of the communications panel had secured their freedom from Drusilla's tyranny, at least for the moment. But they knew with the protective forcefield in place, the alien creatures would not be able to reach them. Harry had wanted to ensure that every single enemy was no longer on board. When they finally disabled the forcefield and made their way to engineering, that was when Harry had discovered Drusilla had fled in a preservation pod. He had hoped to find her unconscious on the bridge and then kill her himself, but right now, he would settle for having his ship back. The bridge, on the other hand, was another matter. In isolating that part of the ship, they had effectively locked themselves out, and it would take someone to crawl through the maintenance ducts, hack their way into the bridge and restore power, before anyone else could re-enter.

Teale had volunteered for the job, but Harry refused. Risking one life was bad enough, but risking a second who had no control over the decision, was out of the question. The conversation garnered a few looks from other crew members who were not yet aware of Teale's condition, but Harry left engineering alone. He found the entrance point where the creatures had torn through the hull with the shields down, and managed to squeeze between the jagged metal and the deck plates to drop down into the bridge. The amount of blood on the floor, turned his stomach, particularly as he had been the cause.

"Necessary evil," he told himself aloud as he made his way to the hidden circuitry beneath the viewscreen.

Removing one of the panels, he sat cross-legged on the floor, and began rearranging chips and wires much as he had done in the cargo bay. Only this time, the job was infinitely more complex. One false connection, and in it's current preservation mode, the bridge would launch all the remaining pods, and deactivate life support.

"Teale to Ransome, how's it going Sir?"

Harry tapped his communicator, a laser scalpel clenched between his teeth.

"Almost there Commander. I've managed to bypass the bulkhead lockouts, and deactivate the security fields. Should have bridge control back in a few minutes."

But then, another siren began wailing throughout the bridge. Harry leapt up and sprinted for the nearest console, forgetting all of his wounds and injuries, and almost collapsing as he did so. Harry had managed to restore power to the science station, and when the problem became evident, his heart sank.

The sensors revealed that the *Odyssey* was caught in a gravitational field, of a strength usually associated with a planetary body. But there was nothing out there. The engines were not yet functioning, and hull stress was increasing.

"Shit!"

Harry flew back down to the communicator he had left by the open access panel.

"Teale? Can you get the engines started?"

"Activating them now Sir, but the pull is too strong!"

"Are they at max?"

"Aye Admiral. When we shorted out the bridge, we lost a few other systems. We're running on everything we've got. The computer estimates three minutes until structural integrity reaches critical levels!"

Think, Harry, think...

His mind flew back to a training scenario back in the design process. There had been significant concern that one of the ships may encounter a gravity well, or be caught in the grip of a black hole. After all, their flight path would take them perilously close to previously discovered phenomenon.

"There may be a way, Jennifer," Harry said solemnly.

Teale had been one of those at the design briefing. She had already considered this plan and dismissed it.

"No you fucking don't! We can find another way!" she yelled down the comms channel.

But they were out of time.

"Do me a favour," Harry asked, a small smile spreading across his face. "Make sure when you get back to Azanti Prime, you make a good life for yourself. And give that baby a good life. For Joshua."

"Harry, please don't do this! You can detach the bridge module, that might give the thrust we need!"

"You and I both know that's not true," Harry replied, frantically switching the wires around. "Your orders are to take this ship to the asteroid belt on the edge of the Azanti system... and leave her there. Do your best to hack into Drusilla's messages and delete them, but if you can't, take a shuttle to Azanti Prime, and live your lives."

As Harry made the necessary final alterations to the panel configuration. A tear fell down his cheek.

"And Jennifer?"

"Yes Harry?"

"Make it a good one."

One press of a button was all it took. The viewscreen broke apart into two vast, glass doors exposing the bridge to open space. The speed at which the bridge decompressed gave the *Odyssey* a surge of extra momentum, and propelled the ship away from the gravity disturbance. Once it was clear, the engines kicked in and the ship blasted away towards safety. As Harry's slowly fading body spiralled down into the black oblivion, he saw his ship disappear out of sight. Icicles formed around his eyes, his lips, and he could feel his blood freezing over. But despite all of this, as the life left his body, once again, he smiled.

TWENTY-ONE

THE CONSTANT BEEP of the medical machine felt as if it was boring into her brain. It had been an ever present noise now for almost two years, but up until now, she had not been able to break free of her coma in order to silence it. But today was different. She could feel the cloth beneath her body, the fibres brushing against her skin. A light breeze flowed over her lips, and as she took in a large lungful of air, she opened her eyes. The lights were bright, and they hurt causing her to blink rapidly for several minutes, trying to adjust.

"Hey there, take it easy, take it easy."

A soothing voice to her side made her turn her head to the left. Sat beside her was a humanoid female, typing commands into a computer tablet. The woman had distinctive markings on her nose, and along her forehead that she had never seen before. Although, at this point, she could not recall any memory of what she had and hadn't encountered before today. The effect was most disarming.

"How do you feel?" asked the alien doctor.

She thought about this for a moment, and felt her dry throat crack as she tried to speak to no avail.

"Hold on, let me help."

The doctor helped her take a large sip of water, the liquid instantly soothing the pains and dryness. She tried again.

"Like I swallowed a bucket of razor blades."

The doctor smiled.

"Your recovery has been long, but the speed you have progressed in the last few days has been nothing short of remarkable. It's as if your brain has lain dormant for all this time, and is now able to reactivate. In truth, we have done nothing but keep you comfortable."

She allowed the words to sink in, but barely understood them. All this time? How long was that. Thankfully she did not have to wait too long for a response to that one.

"You've been our most popular patient since you came in here two years ago. Everybody is curious about where you came from. We have never seen another being like yourself."

Two years.

"Where... where am I? Where did you find me?"

The doctor checked her notes.

"Your pod was found by a farmer in one of his crop fields. Much of it was lost in the initial fire by the time he found you. You'd been thrown from the pod several hundred feet. How you had no broken bones, I have no idea. You've been in a coma ever since. Until today."

Pod. Crashed. These words meant something to her, but her mind could not yet organise the thoughts. But then a far more troubling notion sprang to the surface.

"Who- who am I?" she asked.

The doctor nodded sympathetically, and reached into the pocket of her lab coat.

"When the farmer found you, you had this scrap of identification on you. It's mostly faded away, but it has your picture, and a first name. Drusilla. Does that sound familiar?"

In truth, it did not. She did not know who she was, and had no recollection of her name whatsoever. But the picture was undeniably her. There was a small logo in the corner of what looked like a damaged ID card of some sort. It was a blue and green planet that she did not recognise, and the word 'Utopia'. She had no memories of the card nor how she came to possess it,

"As for your family name, the pod you were found in was lost, as I say. But there was a name detailed on the side, I presume the pods were personalised."

Trying to make sense of it all, she asked the doctor, "What was the name?"

"Ransome."

Again, there was no realisation attached to that name. But at least she had something to call herself. She nodded to the doctor, who told her to get some more rest and they would try and find her some food. After the doctor left, her mind raced for a while, as she tried to grasp any semblance of who she was or where she had come from. There was also a nagging itch at the back of her mind. The room appeared to be filled with chattering and whispers, but the other patients in the ward appeared to be quiet or speaking at a reduced volume. Somehow, she could hear several of them clearly. Moments later, another hospital orderly arrived, holding a piece of card.

"Ah it's good to see you up and awake! I've come to ask what you would like for lunch, Miss...?"

She thought for a moment.

"Ransome. Drusilla Ransome."

EPILOGUE

IT WAS the harsh breeze that jolted him awake. It was like icicles tearing into his skin. As his eyes flew open, he realised that not only was he freezing cold, but he was also very much naked. As his eyes adjusted to the dim light in the room, he discovered he was lying on a metal table of some kind, and there was a trolley full of instruments off to his left. A distant drip, drip, drip from a pipe somewhere, sent a dull echo around the room.

"Where the fuck..."

"Ah, you are awake! Excellent. That means we have made progress!"

A rather excited gentleman in a long white lab coat burst through a plastic curtain at the far end of the room, and it was only when Harry moved to stand up, he realised he was being held down on the table by restraints around his chest, both arms and his legs.

"Just what the hell is going on here!" Harry shouted, his throat raw, his voice jagged.

The man removed his goggles, and rolled a chair to the edge of the table, sitting in it and leaning in towards Harry's face.

"Well, would you like the short answer, or the long answer?"

Harry had never wanted to punch someone in the face so hard in his entire life.

"Allow me to give you the short answer, then."

The man got up from his chair, and began pacing the room, tapping a pen on his wrist as he walked from one side of the room to the other, methodically.

"My name is Doctor Tim Blakeman. I was placed here entirely by accident, oh about... ninety years ago. Give or take."

Ninety years? Harry was astonished. The man did not look a day over forty, and he was almost certainly human. The confusion clouded his vision, and he had to focus to hear the rest of the words.

"You see, long before your time Admiral, a small group of us were working on a significantly advanced form of artificial life. Far beyond that of artificial intelligence, you understand. Something much more intricate and unique. Of course those on Earth with morals and objections caused our research to be shut down before we even started. But someone came to me, and offered me a chance to continue my work. I believe she is a mutual friend of yours."

Drusilla. Fucking bitch, Harry thought.

"Anyway, she got a little, shall we say, trigger happy with my associates, and so I, and there's no easy way to say this, stole her ship and ran away."

Harry almost laughed at that one. The idea of anyone successfully stealing a ship from Drusilla filled him with joy.

"I managed to barter and trade my way to the Saraswathi System, and I discovered a wonderful spatial phenomenon. I did not have the means to fully explore it, but it appeared to be some kind of energy nebula. I tried to get close to it, but I couldn't penetrate the perimeter, the ship was too weak after several skirmishes and lack of good maintenance on my part. I lost control, and found myself crashing on this frozen planet you currently find yourself on. It is quite fortunate I had made the discoveries I had before the accident, or I would be very much dead, and my research lost forever."

Harry did not like where this was going. As feared, this was definitely a laboratory, and not a medical facility. He had to know.

"How long have I been here?"

Looking slightly offended at being interrupted, Blakeman sighed and gave the response.

"You fell from the sky roughly five years ago. And there wasn't much of you left after the impact, I can tell you that much!"

Five years. How could that be? And then a dormant thought came rushing to the fore like a flood in his mind.

"The gravitational field? It was this planet?"

Blakeman was animated once more.

"Ah yes! Another one of my genius inventions. You see, I was fortunate to have basically a whole laboratory onboard the ship I stole, and when I landed here, this facility was abandoned, and so I've been tinkering away perfecting my craft for quite some time now. You are a shining example of that. The perception filter is another."

"Perception filter? You mean like a cloaking device?"

"Yes! Precisely!"

But now was time to focus on the other part of Blakeman's statement.

"I am an example of your work?"

Blakeman nodded enthusiastically.

"Oh yes my friend. The artificial lifeforms I have spent almost a century working on, undoubtedly saved your life. You've basically been reconstructed from the DNA upwards. I am so very proud of my little autonomous children."

Even though it wasn't possible to get any colder than he was,

Harry shivered. The demeanour, the words, the actions of this so called doctor, chilled Harry to the core. He couldn't speak, the words caught like a lump in the throat. But he needn't bother. Because Blakeman spoke first.

"Alas, although you are awake, the task is not yet completed. There is more work to be done. I think... yes... spinal fusion should be our next task. Don't you think so my little beauties?"

Blakeman turned towards a large cabinet. Inside were several vials of various coloured liquids and equipment. But the specimen jar in the centre, larger than all of the others, contained some kind of swirling mass. A soft green glow came from whatever the creature was, and as Harry watched on, Blakeman reached into the cabinet and extracted the jar. He carried it over to Harry's restrained form, and unscrewed the lid.

"Oh yes, soon we will have you better than new, Admiral."

He grabbed Harry's jaw, and squeezed his mouth open, and gently tilted the jar forwards. In one smooth motion, the creature inside the jar plunged down Harry's throat, his body convulsing violently. As Blakeman screwed on the jar's lid and walked away, Harry Ransome's screams echoed throughout the entire facility, and across the entire frozen world.